Digenis
Akritas

Digenis Akritas

THE TWO-BLOOD BORDER LORD

The Grottaferrata Version

*Translated with
an Introduction
and Notes by*
DENISON B. HULL

OHIO UNIVERSITY PRESS
ATHENS, OHIO

*f*OR MY CHILDREN

Contents

Preface

SEVERAL years ago while attending a luncheon in the gardens of Dumbarton Oaks in Washington, where the Center for Byzantine Studies is located, I ran across an old friend, Leon Zach, then president of the American Society of Landscape Architects. He offered to show me around, explaining that he knew every inch of the gardens because he was responsible for seeing that they were kept up. When we had finished looking around, I congratulated him, and remarked that I envied him for having such a pleasant place to work.

"Maybe I should study Byzantine Greek," I added, "Then I could work here too."

"No," he said, shaking his head. "You couldn't. You'd have to spend most of the year working in Cambridge."

He did not say, "studying theology," but that is what my imagination supplied, for I had always had the impression that Byzantine literature was a Sahara filled with dry ecclesiastical histories and hairsplitting arguments on dogma. These have their purposes, of course, but they are not a part of my world. With this thought in mind, I looked around, half expecting to see students clad in the long black garments and flat hats of the Roman seminaries. I had forgotten for the moment that it was spring vacation and that all the students were away. I was just as glad not to see them; I envied them the use of the place, but I was sure their life was not the life I wanted to lead in a garden like that. Anyway my mind was closed. I knew that Byzantine literature was not for me, even if I were qualified to work in the Center, and I was not. So I dismissed the subject from my mind.

Then one day, while reading William McNeill's *The Rise of the West*, I came across a reference to an epic poem called *Digenis*

Akritas, written in medieval Greek in about the eleventh century. A poem? An epic, and not just another hymn? In medieval Greek? My curiosity was aroused, for it had never occurred to me that such a piece existed. I was curious too about the eleventh-century Greek; I knew a little of the ancient tongue and had taken some lessons in the modern. I was anxious to see what lay between. I looked in the encyclopedia, and to my surprise I found the entry, DIGENES AKRITAS, BASILIUS, Byzantine national hero of about the tenth century. I didn't remember seeing this name in Gibbon's *Decline and Fall of the Roman Empire,* so I looked, and just as I had expected, it was not there. I intended to check the card catalog at the library of the University of Chicago but before I had a chance to look, I ran into Kimon Friar the translator of Kazantzakis' enormous modern Greek epic, *The Odyssey, a Modern Sequel,* and asked him if he had heard of *Digenis Akritas.*

"Of course!" he answered. "Every Greek has heard of it!"

"I suppose it's hard to find a copy in this country," I said, foolishly assuming that if neither Gibbon nor I had ever heard of it, the library hadn't either.

"On the contrary," he said, "it's easy. You can order a copy through any good book store. The Oxford University Press has published a new edition."

I ordered a copy, and the moment it came, I sat down and began to read it. In a very short time I learned three things. First, the poem had been known in western Europe since 1875, long enough ago for many scholars to make notes and commentaries on it in Latin, German, French, Italian, and, of course, in modern Greek. There was even a Russian version of it. Obviously I would be hard put to add much to the store of knowledge already accumulated. But second, the poem badly needed a literary translation that would make it known to English-speaking people who know no Greek. There was indeed a literal translation of it in the book I bought, but in many places (Book 7, lines 171-73, for instance) it is practically unintelligible without the aid of the Greek. The truth is that the editor, John Mavrogordato, attempted the impossible, a word-for-word, line-for-line translation in normal English word order, in five stress iambic lines with a vocabulary of words taken, so he says, from the King

James Version of the Bible, Shakespeare, Milton and the 16th century ballads. As any experienced translator could have foreseen, one or all of these requirements had to give way. The good professor knows and loves his Greek, loves the poem and understands its background very well. His book has been invaluable to me. It is a splendid piece of scholarship, well ahead of most of the rest of us. But the translation gives very little idea of what the poem is like. When I read the Greek, I discovered the third thing, Byzantine Greek is no more difficult than any other Greek. Some words that look familiar have acquired strange meanings, and some words of foreign origin are just plain strange, but all can be interpreted with the aid of a few easily obtainable lexicons, or through the footnotes in one or another of the texts; many can be guessed from the context.

Anyway I have put the poem into English blank verse, knowing full well that translation is treason, but hoping nevertheless that I may be able to give the reader some small idea of its charm in Greek. This poem, of course, has its weaknesses; no one would call it dramatic, and it has its share of prosy narrative passages and bits of silliness. But it has endured for nearly a thousand years in the hearts of the Greeks not only because it celebrates the Orthodoxy of the Greek people, but also because it has charm, because there is music in its lines, and because the scenes it depicts of life on the frontier of the Eastern Empire, the Greek empire, when men like Basil were struggling to hold back the barbarians who threatened to destroy it, are beautiful, resembling quaint old tapestries or frescoes, and often shining with the rich glitter of gold mosaic. As it is impossible to attempt a reconstruction of the original *Digenis Akritas,* it was necessary to choose which version to translate. Many versions were disqualified by incompleteness or by remoteness, only two were considered, the Andros and the Grottaferrata versions. We have chosen the latter in the belief that it is of higher literary quality than the Andros.

In selecting the appropriate English verse form, it seemed best to choose one that occupies the same position in English poetry that the political verse occupies in Greek. Three possibilities existed. The seven-stress iambic line of the English ballads closely resembles the Greek; however, it is associated in English with light or humorous verse, and it is too long to use on a line-for-line basis without the necessity of considerable "stuffing." We had already decided on a line-for-line basis to keep the same proportion and emphasis in the translation as in the original poem. Of the two verse forms that were suitable, the rhymed couplet, usually known as the heroic couplet, and blank verse, the rhymed couplet would give a pithy, succinct quality reminding the reader of aphorisms and epitaphs; but each couplet is a unit, and enjambment is difficult. The story cannot flow, but must be chopped up into a number of separate units. A few experiments with blank verse, however, proved that five-stress iambic lines were almost a perfect length for keeping the translation on a line-for-line basis. Frequently a weak eleventh syllable has been added, either by tucking it in the middle of a line where it almost disappears, or by putting it at the end of the line to give a feminine ending. Pressure to keep the lines short compelled the use of concise modern English and taut sentence structure, and occasionally the dropping of a weak adjective. There are a few small archaisms like "lest" or "ere," but no nineteenth-century poeticisms like "o'er" and "e'er." The traditional English practice of using the old and otherwise obsolete second person singular in addressing the Deity has been followed.

I wish to thank the nice people who have given generous help, advice and encouragement to me. I should never have been able to finish this book without them. They are:

Constantine A. Trypanis, formerly Bywater and Sotheby Professor of Byzantine and Modern Greek Literature and Language, Oxford University, and now University Professor of Classical Languages and Literatures, the University of Chicago; Mary P. Gianos, Professor and Chairman of the Division of the Humanities, Detroit Institute of Technology, and Editor, TWAS, Greek Authors series; Herman Fussler, Director of the University Library and Professor in the Graduate Library School, the University of Chicago; Francis R. Walton, Librarian of the Gennadius Library, American School of Classical Studies, Athens; Reuben A. Brower, Professor of English, and Honorary Associate and former Master of Adams House, Harvard University; and John Hawthorne, Associate Professor of Classical Languages in the College, the University of Chicago. I wish also to acknowledge the courtesy of Houghton Mifflin Company, publishers of *The Complete Poetical Works of Spenser* and *The Complete Poetical Works of John Milton,* and Douglas Bush, Gurney Professor Emeritus of English at Harvard, editor of Milton.

These people have all been so willing, cheerful and friendly that I hope no one will blame them for the mistakes, which are wholly mine. Much credit for what I have learned is due them.

Introduction

BASIL the Two-Blood Border Lord, better known by his Greek name, Basileios Digenis Akritas, was a legendary hero of the Byzantine Empire, a gigantic figure clad in Christian orthodoxy, who has become the symbol of the eternal spirit of Hellas to the modern Greeks. His story, commonly known as *Digenis Akritas*, follows in many respects the same epic tradition as the *Iliad*, the *Morte Darthur*, the *Chanson de Roland*, and the *Nibelungenlied*, which honor national heroes, were written long after the event, and contain threads of recognizable history. Like these epics, the story of Basil the Two-Blood Border Lord contains the theme of loyalty to a code of honor and behavior, although its code is somewhat different. In order to understand and enjoy this Byzantine poem, one must become acquainted with the Byzantine point of view. As we can only give a very superficial description of Byzantine life and literature in this introduction, we suggest J. B. Bury's introduction to the 1923 edition of *The Cambridge Medieval History*, vol. 4, *The Byzantine Empire*, which also has been reproduced in both Part I and Part II of the 1969 edition, edited by J. M. Hussey. Chapters 3, 4, 11, 20, 27, 28 and 30 are pertinent also. "Greek Literature; II Byzantine" by Karl Krumbacher and Franz Sherrard's *Constantinople, Iconography of a Sacred City* (London: Oxford University Press, 1965) best gives the atmosphere of the poem's environment.

Historical Background. The action in the poem occurs during the second half of the ninth century and the first half of the tenth in the Eastern Roman, or Byzantine Empire, particularly that part which lies in Asia Minor around the Taurus Mountains and the Euphrates

River. The Roman Empire (to give it its proper name) at that time, although legally the same empire as that founded by Augustus nearly a thousand years earlier, consisted only of the southern tip of Italy, the eastern shore of Sicily, the Balkan peninsula, and about two-thirds of Asia Minor. It was Roman in name and tradition only, for its capital was Constantinople, its language Greek, and its religion Orthodox Christianity. The original Roman Empire, because of its enormous size, had been divided into two parts for administrative convenience. The Emperor Constantine the Great had founded a new capital for the eastern half on the site of the ancient Greek city of Byzantium at the southern end of the Bosporus, and himself embraced Christianity. Half a century later the Emperor Theodosius made Christianity the official religion of the state, and soon afterwards the western half of the empire fell to the barbarians. The Eastern Roman, or as we now call it, the Byzantine Empire, therefore remained the sole defender of the Christian faith, the center of the civilized world, and a great power, for the name Rome still held magic. Its gold coin, the bezant, dominated finance and commerce throughout Europe and the Mediterranean world and maintained its value for over seven hundred years. The Sacred Palace of its Emperors was so splendid that it vied with the palace of Haroun al-Rashid in Baghdad, so vividly described for us in the *Thousand and One Nights*. And finally, Byzantium was the repository of all the learning of the past, the books and treasures of the classical world.

In a state with a centralized government such as that of the Byzantine Empire, where a huge bureaucracy existed, the road to advancement was solely through education, particularly a Hellenistic education. Any foreigner, whether Slav or Arab, could become a Byzantine simply by submission to the Emperor and conversion to the Orthodox faith, but the upper classes who occupied most of the offices in the bureaucracy were Greek, and both proud and jealous of their Hellenism. An education on the classical model was therefore essential, not for cultural reasons alone, but for economic reasons as well. Opportunities for learning were excellent. In Constantinople at the secular university in the Magnaura Palace, founded in 864, Leo the Mathematician, the man who built the famous golden plane tree with its mechanical singing birds and roaring lions in the throne room for the Emperor Theophilus, taught philosophy, higher arithmetic, music, geometry and astronomy, and all students were expected to be thoroughly versed in the classics and rhetoric. Thus, at a time when only the clergy and a few traders in western Europe knew how to read and write, the upper-class Byzantines could swap quotations from Homer and the classics, or argue fine points of theological doctrine. Even in the provinces education was not wholly ignored. If the military aristocracy on its big estates could barely write a sentence that was free from elementary mistakes in spelling and grammar, even the poorest child could learn to read and write if he were determined. The Church, at the Third Council of Constantinople in 681, had ordained that the clergy should establish church schools in all towns and villages to teach elementary subjects that were economically necessary, and some of these, at least, must still have been in operation in the ninth and tenth centuries.

But the central fact of the Empire was the Emperor himself. He was not only the legitimate heir to the throne of the ancient Roman Empire, still the most powerful single state in Europe, but more important, he was considered God's representative on earth. He governed by the grace of God; his imperial power proceeded from God's grace. If he were murdered, it was a sign that God's grace had abandoned him. If his murderer succeeded him to the throne, God's grace apparently had descended on the murderer. The Emperor was not deified, as the pagan emperors had been, although Constantine had been given the title Equal to the Apostles and was thought to be the wisest of the heralds of the faith—one who, with Christ as his breastplate, could deflect the weapons of the enemy.

And the empire had many enemies. The German, Viking, Slavic, Hunnish and Turkic migrations during the fourth and fifth centuries were over, but they had left a turbulence and unrest in their wakes, for many tribes were still looking for permanent places to settle. The Empire was therefore in constant danger of being overrun, particularly from the north and east, the directions from which the latest migrants had come. The west was still Roman in culture and sentiment; the empire founded by Charlemagne on the ruins of the old Western Roman Empire was in convulsions for some time after his death, and the new German states of western Europe were still not strong enough to make trouble. The Normans would not begin their conquest of southern Italy and Sicily for another hundred years, and the struggle between the Emperor and the Pope for control of the Church had not yet reached the breaking point. The Arabs under Maslama had tried to take Constantinople in 717 but had lost 150,000 men out of an army of 180,000 and all but five of a fleet of 2,500 ships, which had been burned by Greek fire, the secret weapon of the Byzantines, or had been sunk in action or wrecked by storms. The Slavs had infiltrated the central part of the Balkan peninsula, and the Bulgars had tried several times to take the city by land, but had failed. They were the most dangerous enemy the Empire had on its northern frontier. At the time the events in the poem begin, Krum, their Sublime Khan, had just died, and his successor, Omortag, had concluded a thirty years' peace with Byzantium.

The worst threat at this time came, as it so often did, from the east, not from the Persians, their historic enemies, who had been permanently crushed by the Emperor Heraclius in the seventh century, nor from the Ottoman Turks, who had not yet appeared on the scene, but from the Arabs. Ever since the Prophet Mohammed had proclaimed Islam, the Arabs had been conducting a never-ending holy war; practically, there might be truces at any time because the state of active combat did not exist everywhere simultaneously and individual Arabs and Byzantines might become friendly. But the Prophet himself had made it a practice to raid enemy territory at least once a year. The Caliphs who succeeded him increased the number of raids to two, or sometimes three. The spring raid was usually conducted between May 10 and June 10, and lasted about thirty days. The summer raid was between July 10 and September 8, and lasted about sixty days. The third raid was in winter, and lasted about twenty days during February and March.

To meet these threats the emperor had a well-equipped, well-organized, well-trained, and well-disciplined army. It bore little resemblance to the infantry legions of pagan Rome, for it consisted largely of heavy cavalry used in mass formation, and infantry, though still in use, was only an auxiliary. In addition it had a form of field artillery, catapults mounted on carts, which were used for throwing stones or showers of arrows. In the field each army had its own baggage train and a well-organized medical service, as well as a sort of chaplains' corps, a body of orators, who accompanied the troops to encourage them in battle. Military handbooks such as the *Strategicon* attributed to the Emperor Maurice, the *Tacticon* of Leo VI, and the *Strategicon* of Kekaumenos make it clear that nothing was left to chance that might be provided for by planning. When a Byzantine army lost a battle, it was not for lack of skill or courage, but owing to the bad judgment of the general, such as that of Romanus IV Diogenes, who, in spite of courage and will to win, lost the battle of Manzikert by judgment that was unfortunate, to say the least.

At the time of Basil the Two-Blood Border Lord troops were recruited by giving them hereditary military landholdings in return for their service. This system worked well; it facilitated recruiting because the men had a personal stake in the empire. The army was recruited from and stationed in the *themes,* or military districts, into which the empire had been divided both for military purposes and for civil administration. In addition there were a number of small military districts called *kleisurai* intended to guard the mountain passes, many of which later became themes. Each theme, with a few special exceptions, was commanded by a *strategos,* or general, who was both its military commander and its civil administrator. Finally, there were the *akritai,* the border troops, successors to the pagan Roman *limitanei,* whose duty it was to engage in the actual day-by-day petty warfare with infidels and outlaws. Originally the akritai had been no more than armed peasants settled on the border for protection. In Basil's time, however, they were organized as an independent force, stationed in a series of strongpoints, each with its own officers, of whom Basil was probably one, and normally independent of the general of the adjacent theme. Each such strongpoint was provided with a beacon for signaling in order to keep in touch with the others; in fact there was a series of such beacons reaching all the way from the Taurus Mountains to the Bosporus in order to keep the emperor, seated by his window in the palace, informed of all that happened on the border.

Literary Background. The Byzantines were well aware and exceedingly proud that their empire was the sole defender of the Christian faith and the center of the civilized world. They knew that the capital Constantinople was not only one of the largest cities in the world, but also the most magnificent, as was proper for the Sacred City of the Mother of God, the special care of the Virgin, a city under Her protection. They knew that their emperor was God's vicegerent and representative on earth, deriving his power from the grace of God, and ruling with God. And they were supremely conscious that their own language, Greek, was the language in which all the great poets, dramatists, historians, and philosophers of antiquity had written. More important still, they knew that God himself had given His final revelation the New Testament to mankind in the Greek tongue. As the boundaries of human knowledge could never be extended further by man, least of all by the barbarians beyond the frontier, the Byzantines felt that they had a sacred duty not only to make God's revelation known throughout the world, unchanged and perfect in its wisdom, and to protect and preserve both the sacred writings and the heritage of their forefathers, but also to keep the Greek language itself unchanged and uncorrupted in its purity for all eternity.

The first of these duties was not difficult. Since there was no use exploring the nature of man and his world further, they were able to concentrate all their efforts on copying, editing and commenting, interpreting dogma, and codifying literary forms. If it seems to us today that they produced relatively little of great originality, we can still be grateful that they performed the important task of preserving the very ideas which were later to inspire the new humanism of the Renaissance and of the Enlightenment in western Europe. But the second task was already complicated by the dichotomy which had appeared in the Greek language. The written and the spoken tongues were no longer the same. There had been no such difficulty in antiquity: both tongues were the same, and the spelling of both was phonetic, whether written or spoken in the Attic, Old Ionic, Ionic, Doric, or Aeolic dialects, all of which, in spite of noticeable differences, were mutually intelligible. What caused this dichotomy, however, was not the dialectal differences but the fact that the Attic dialect had become dominant during the period of Athenian supremacy and had been disseminated throughout the east during the conquests of Alexander. This dialect, the Koiné, or common dialect, was the form of Greek spoken throughout the eastern half of the Roman Empire and by all cultured people in the west as well. But owing to the influence of the native tongues of the barbarians, whose lands had been annexed to the empire, pronunciation changed, and grammatical forms sometimes became indistinguishable, and had to be simplified.

Yet all this time the written language under the influence of the Church and the pride of the Hellenic people who formed the governing classes remained unchanged, or, if anything, became ever more rigidly Attic. It was the tongue of government, of scholars, bookmen and churchmen; and everything of importance was written in it. Poets continued to write in the old classical forms, adhering to the principles of quantitative meter laid down by the ancients. In time, of course, the changed pronunciation of the language changed the rhythms of the language, and by the seventh and eighth centuries poets like George Pisides attempted to obtain rhythmic effects based on stressed syllables, though still adhering to the old rules of prosody. It was a worthy attempt but it was bound to fail because it was both difficult and artificial. A new freedom was needed, which could only come with the abandonment of classical prosody. Fortunately as the old forms of writing declined, new forms were developed from the speech of the peasants, who had created their own folk tales and folk songs in the spoken tongue. All sorts of material was used, some of it written, and much of it oral. When a legend began to grow up around a man, singers began to compose songs about him from whatever material they had at hand. Each singer felt that it was part of his art to improve not only on his predecessors, but on his own previous performances, so that the songs continued to grow and to diversify until eventually someone, perhaps the singers themselves, but probably scribes, wrote them down. Thereafter each song suffered the usual alterations that occur to all literature.

Each version of *Digenis Akritas,* therefore, is built up in several layers. The first is the episode on which the legend is based; the second is the accretion of source material, written and oral, attached to it; the third is the embroidery, consisting sometimes of complete stories grafted on, which the bards added to improve their performances; fourth is the layer of corrections, alterations and errors committed by the scribes who copied the earliest written version. It is not suprising therefore that *Digenis Akritas* can be found in several versions, and that it is impossible to reconstruct its archetype. There was no archetype. For a better understanding of the oral tradition of poetry than can be given here, see Albert Lord's *The Singer of Tales* (New York: Atheneum, 1965).

Sources. The materials available to the singer who composed our version of *Digenis Akritas* were many and varied. He had Homer and the classics, the Septuagint and the New Testament, local legends of the Philopappi, the kings of the ancient kingdom of Commagene, whose capital was Samosata, where it is possible that our poet lived. He had tales from the *Thousand and One Nights,* perhaps in the Arabic versions, but probably in the Persian sources; he may have had Firdausi's *Shah Namah,* or its Pahlavi prototype; he had the Turkish epic *Saïd Battal,* from which at least one name in the poem was borrowed. He might have had St. John Damascene's *Barlaam and Ioasaph,* but there is no evidence in the Grottaferrata version that he had read it, although his counterpart, the composer of the Andros version, seems to have borrowed a seer and the concept of the imprisoned child from it. An finally, he had the Hellenistic romances, the *Chaereas and Callirhoe* of Chariton, the *Ephesiaca* of Xenophon of Ephesus, the *Aethiopica* of Heliodorus, the *Leucippe and Cleitophon* of Achilles Tatius, and the *Romance of Alexander*—not Arrian's history, but the work of the pseudo-Callisthenes of about A.D. 300.

It is evident at first glance that the author borrowed nothing of plot or pattern from the classics. Where the *Odyssey* begins in the middle and then goes back to explain how Odysseus happened to land on the shore of Scheria, *Digenis Akritas* begins before Basil's birth and ends at his funeral. The author borrowed nothing of plot from the romances either. The romances are cinematographic in movement, complex in plot, full of characters, and usually involve much travel and many adventures. They are love stories in which virtue always triumphs. *Digenis Akritas is* slow moving, simple in plot, contains few characters, and is deeply religious. It is episodic, lacks drama, and is encomiastic. Chariton's story is a historical novel because many

[xxii]

of the characters are real people acting as they did in history; *Digenis Akritas* contains people who may be historical, but cannot be positively identified by their actions. The story of Xenophon of Ephesus is very much concerned with religion—the religion of Artemis; *Digenis Akritas* is strongly Orthodox Christian. Longus' poem is pastoral; *Digenis Akritas* is concerned only with the high nobility and a few outlaws.

The truth is that both the classics and the romances are used as sources of color and decoration only, and what action there is comes from local legends like those of the Philopappi. Generally, source material is used to give verisimilitude to the poem. For this purpose shadowy figures which seem to come from history are scattered throughout the poem. A great deal of effort has been made by many first-class scholars to identify them, but in reality they are only paper dolls cut out from history books and pasted onto the pages of the poem. Who, for instance, is the Emperor? He is named Basil in the Grottaferrata version and also in the Slavic version. But which Basil? He cannot be Basil I the Macedonian c.918-80 if he sent Antakinos-Andronicus Ducas into exile; historically Andronicus Ducas defected during the reign of Leo VI. He cannot be Basil II the Bulgar-slayer c.958-1025, who lived long after the Emir became Christian. He is called Romanus in other texts, but historically he cannot have been Romanus I, II or III. His name is simply borrowed from history.

But if the identity of the Emperor is uncertain, the identity of Basil the Two-Blood Border Lord is nearly impossible to determine. For historical reasons he cannot have been either emperor of that name although he has characteristics in common with each. In appearance he resembles both Constantine IX Monomachos and George Maniakes. The very idea that he might have been an obscure general named Pantherios whose name was changed for political reasons seems silly to me: names cannot be forgotten quite so easily. He could not have been a good regimental officer named Diogenes because the name Diogenes is not cognate with Digenis, a name which would not have been derived from it. It is true, of course, that the composers of some of the folk songs, misunderstanding the name, and feeling that the accent was on the wrong syllable, did turn it into Digénis, which might have been derived from Diogenes. But Digénis promptly became

Giánnes, and Digenís did not. Moreover, Digenís is a word of scholarly formation, and its root meaning is pointed out clearly in the poem. And finally, he could never have been a regimental officer; he was a lone wolf, a man who walked by himself, as strange and independent as Kipling's cat.

The only other possibility that I can think of is that there was indeed a border soldier named Basil, named, as were many others, for St. Basil of Caesarea. The sanctity associated with the name may have inspired the first bards who sang of this obscure soldier to magnify his character and his deeds into something representative of Christian Orthodoxy. That the name had more than common associations is evident in the attributes attached to the emperor who appears in Grottaferrata version. He is called *blessed* twice (G-iv 56, 973). Romanus and Nicephorus in other versions are called *great, rich, brilliant,* and *conquering,* but never *blessed.* Is it possible that the name had sufficient magic to raise an obscure border soldier to the eminence reached in the poem? It is hard to believe. At any rate the identity of Basil is still an unsolved question. We know only that he was so obscure at first that none of the chroniclers mention him, but he so impressed the imagination of the people that even as late as 1922 during the unfortunate military campaign in Asia Minor, the peasants of Pontus awaited the awakening of Digenis Akritas with his huge mace and terrible war cry.

Theme and Purpose. The ancient Greeks didn't believe in art for art's sake. The proper function of literature, in their opinion, was to instruct. Didactic poetry can be found in all periods of Greek literature, beginning with Hesiod, continuing through Nicander of Colophon, who wrote about antidotes for snakebite, and Oppian (two men, really) who wrote poems on hunting and fishing, to the Hellenistic romances we have already mentioned. Hard as it may be to believe, these frivolous tales had a didactic purpose. Heliodorus extols the dark-skinned Ethiopians, Xenophon of Ephesus shows us that Artemis does not neglect her devotees, and Dio Chrysostom reminds us somewhat of Rousseau when he shows the manner in which the honest rustic outsmarts the city slicker. But was there a didactic purpose behind the story of Basil the Two-Blood Border Lord? Probably not. It is obvious that it was not a defense of Orthodoxy against Iconoclasm; the poet never hints that the empire had been torn by the tragic iconoclastic controversy. It is not a defense of Orthodoxy against the Paulician heresy; the poet never mentions the Paulicians. It is not nationalism or patriotism; the poem is filled with Greeks, Arabs, Armenians, and people of mixed blood—including the hero himself. The whole concept of nationalism as we know it today was unknown then. It is not involved with dynastic or political quarrels; the author seems unaware of such things. It is certainly not historical, and it is not dramatic. The conflicts of character that occur in such things is lacking.

Digenis Akritas is called an epic, but it deserves this name from the stature of its hero, not from his acts. His deeds do not help to develope a plot, but simply to illustrate his character. It is therefore an epic encomium rather than simply an epic, the celebration of Hellenic Orthodoxy rather than of a historic figure. The Hellenism it celebrates is not ethnic but cultural; the Orthodoxy it praises is not exclusive, but all-embracing. It is this combination of Hellenic culture and Orthodox faith that gives the poem its appeal to the Greeks today. In addition the charm of its music and the grace of its pictures give it universal appeal.

Versions and Texts. Because of the methods used in oral composition there is no original version of *Digenis Akritas,* and what we have today are only different versions told by different bards, written down later, and then copied by various scribes. The texts themselves are, of course copies made from earlier copies of the first written texts, but as they are all derived from different oral versions (excepting possibly A and T which may be from the same oral version), it is impossible to reconstruct an archetype. We can, however, determine the content of real history in the poem and shall return to this presently.

There are six versions in Greek, of which five are in verse and one in prose, and one composite version in the Slavonic tongue which was in use during the Kievan period of Russian literature. It is possible that there may have been still other versions in existence as late as the eighteenth century, for Caesar Dapontes, a monk of that time, reported seeing two copies in a monastery on Mount Athos. In addition, there are a large number of folk songs—some of which may very well have had their origin in other versions of the poem about which we know nothing—belonging to what is known as the Akritic Cycle, which tell stories related (sometimes very vaguely) to Basil and his companions.

At any rate, what we have today are the following listed (except for the Slavic version) in order of discovery:

1. THE TREBIZOND VERSION (referred to hereafter as T), consists of 3182 lines of verse, and is divided into ten books; the beginning is missing, and there are several small gaps in it. The manuscript was written no earlier than the sixteenth century, and was found by Savvas Ioannides in the monastery of Soumela in Trebizond in 1858. It was published in Paris in 1875 by C. Sathas and E. Legrand, and again in Constantinople in 1887 by Ioannides. The original manuscript is now lost.

2. THE ANDROS VERSION (referred to as A), called the Athens version by P. P. Kalonaros, and placed first in his collection. It consists of 4778 lines of verse, and is divided into ten books; it is very nearly complete, and almost a duplicate of T, so that one may be used to correct the other. The manuscript, written in the sixteenth century, was found in Andros in 1878, and published by A. Meliarakes in 1881. The manuscript is now in the National Library in Athens.

3. THE GROTTAFERRATA VERSION (referred to as G), consists of 3709 lines of verse, and is divided into eight books; it is complete except for a gap in the sixth book where a page has been torn out. The manuscript appears to have been written in the fourteenth century, and although it can hardly be a transcript from the poet's dictation, it is probably very close to it. It was discovered in the Greek rite monastery of Grottaferrata near Frascati, Italy, in 1879, and was published in Paris by E. Legrand in 1892.

4. THE OXFORD VERSION (referred to as O), is a rhymed version in 3094 lines divided into ten books, and signed by the scribe, Ignatios Petritzes, a monk of Chios, who dated his manuscript when he finished it, 25 November, 1670. The manuscript is at Lincoln College, Oxford, and was published by S. Lampros in 1880.

5. THE ESCORIAL VERSION (referred to as E), is incomplete, consisting of only 1867 lines of verse. Its language is somewhat similar to that of the folk songs, but the story is muddled and confused, and the lines are sometimes short, or they are extended into prose. It seems to have been dictated by a very old man who was trying, unsuccessfully, to recall it from memory. The manuscript was found by Karl Krumbacher in 1904, and published by D. C. Hesseling in 1912. It is in the Escorial Library in Madrid.

6. THE PROSE VERSION (referred to as P), in ten books, is little more than a prose version of the Andros manuscript. It was written by Meletios Vlastos of Chios in 1632, discovered by D. Paschales in Andros in 1898, published in 1928, and is now in the library of the department of folklore at the University of Thessaloniki.

7. THE SLAVIC VERSION (referred to as S) was assembled by M. Speransky in 1922 from two eighteenth-century manuscripts and a quotation by the eighteenth-century Russian historian Nikolai Karamzin. The two eighteenth-century manuscripts were written in thirteenth-century Slavonic; the manuscript from which Karamzin took his quotation was burned in Moscow in 1812. It is incomplete. The text was published by Speransky in 1922, translated into French by P. Pascal in 1935, and into modern Greek by Petros P. Kalonaros in 1941.

The following are critical texts:

Kal. P. P. Kalonaros, ed., *Basileios Digenis Akritas,* 2 vols. Athens: Dimitrakou, A.E., 1949, 1942. Vol. I contains text of the Andros version with notes showing variant readings in Trebizond version, general introduction, bibliography, chronological table, notes and index. Vol. II contains texts of Grottaferrata and Escorial versions, selections from folk songs of the Akritic Cycle, translation in modern Greek of the text of the Slavic version, notes and index.

Mav. John Mavrogordato, ed., *Digenes Akrites,* Oxford: The Clarendon Press, 1956. Contains reprint of text of the Grottaferrata version from E. Legrand's *Les Exploits de Digenis Akritas* Paris, 1892, 1902 with literal English translation on facing pages, introduction, commentary, genealogical table, conspectus of versions and episodes, lists of references to Achilles Tatius, Heliodorus and Meliteniotes, index of Greek words, and index to introduction. See bibliography for Akritic folk songs in Greek.

Ant. Meliarakis, ed., *Basileios Digenis Akritas*, Athens: G. I. Basileiou, 1920. Contains text of the Andros version with notes giving variant readings in Trebizond version, a brief introduction, glossary, and index of personal and geographical names.

The Story. An Arabian emir, on one of his semiannual raids on the Byzantine Empire, abducts the daughter of a Greek general. The offspring of their union is Basil, who, because he is born of two races, is called *di-genís,* which is translated Two-Blood on the ground that half-breed and similar terms have a pejorative connotation. Because he becomes a defender of the border, or *akra,* of the Empire, he is called *akrítis,* which became *Akritas,* perhaps on the mistaken assumption that it was a proper name. Basil in turn runs off with the daughter of a Greek general, is married, and lives alone with his wife on the border where he performs astounding feats, builds himself a palace on the banks of the Euphrates River, dies young, and is honored by all the notables of the East.

The story may be divided into two major parts, the story of the emir, and the story of Basil. The second part may be further subdivided into three sections: Basil's youth; Basil's exploits, told by himself; and Basil's death. The second part is a curious double of the first, and there are duplications that raise the suspicion that originally there was only one story.

Language and Prosody. The language of the Grottaferrata version is moderately good literary Greek, resembling in many respects that of the New Testament, although the manuscript is marred with many misspellings and errors of punctuation, accentuation and breathing, probably due to the ignorance of the scribe who copied it. When compared with the language of the New Testament, however, the trend toward the modern spoken tongue is apparent. The infinitive of indirect discourse with the subject in the accusative is not utterly lacking, but is infrequent; participial absolutes are sometimes in the nominative rather than in the classical genitive; the use of ὡς with the subjunctive instead of the imperative, is common, although it does not wholly replace it; νά (for ancient ἵνα), usually replaces ὅπως and ὡς before final purpose clauses. The vocabulary still resembles the ancient, although there are shifts in the meaning of familiar words, such as ἡλικία for stature, instead of youth; and new dialectal neuter forms, such as ἀδελφίν for sister, are beginning to appear. The language of the other versions is considerably more developed in the direction of the modern spoken tongue, not so much in vocabulary as in grammar and syntax.

The prosody of all versions, however, is well on the way to becoming modern. Excluding the Proem of the Grottaferrata version and lines 261-78 of the Andros version, all are written in unrhymed accentual lines of fifteen syllables, a form known as political verse. There is reason to suspect that this form had its origin in the classical iambic tetrameter catalectic, generally, but not exclusively found in comedy. It has been, and still is the most common form of Greek popular verse and closely resembles the English ballad meter, which, however, usually has one less syllable, and is rhymed. A good example of the fifteen syllable line in English can be found in one of *The Bab Ballads*, "The Periwinkle Girl," by W. S. Gilbert:

I've óften thoúght that heádstrong yoúths / Of décent edúcátion,
Detérmine áll-impórtant trúths / With stránge precípitátion.

Although this is normally written in four lines, I have given it here in two to show the similarity to the Greek, which is not rhymed. Expressed in the usual symbols of macron and breve, the typical line would be represented:

$$|\cup-\cup-|\cup-\cup-|\cup-\cup-|\cup-\cup|$$

The final metron is almost always the same, but the others vary:

1. $|-\cup-\cup|$ 2. $|-\cup\cup-|$ 3. $|\cup--\cup|$.

There are some lines that fit none of these metra, as they are either over, or short, a syllable. These shown however are the commonest.

The English counterpart of lines 261-78 of the Andros version can be found in another of *The Bab Ballads*, "Captain Reece." It begins:

> Of áll the shíps upon the blúe, / No shíp contaíned a bétter créw
> Than thát of wórthy Cáptain Reéce / Commánding óf *The Mántelpiece.*

This example is even closer to the pattern of the Greek than the other, for the Greek rhymes in the same fashion.

Finding a counterpart of the verse form of the Proem of the Grottaferrata version is difficult for two reasons: first, twelve-syllable lines are not common in English, especially trochaic lines and second, the Greek is really written in a debased form of the classical iambic trimeter on quantitative principles with almost unlimited power of substituting alternate forms of feet. Actually iambics predominate. Read accentually, however, it scans more nearly as if it were written in trochaic lines of six stresses. Two examples of English lines will suffice, one to show the quantitative form, and the other the accentual. The first is from book 1, canto 1, of Edmund Spenser's *Faerie Queene*: p.xxx

> |As one for knight|-ly giusts and fierce| en-coun-ters fitt.|

This is marked as if it were quantitative, but it is really a six-stress iambic line, called an alexandrine. It will not divide up into three metra without breaking into a word, and for that reason alone is a poor example.

The second example is a six-stress trochaic line, a form almost unknown in English. As the rhythm is similar to Longfellow's *Hiawatha*, the following example will have to suffice:

> Híawátha hád a líne a líttle shórter.

The Greek poet was trying to combine both rhythms.

Oral Tradition: Formulas. The presence in a poem of repeated phrases, lines, and groups of two or more lines is evidence that oral methods may have entered into its composition and transmission. In the G version alone the following examples of formulas can be found:

1. the land of Heracles. G-i 50
the land of Heracles, G-iv 41
2. the three mile mark. G-ii 298
within three miles G-iv 800
the three mile mark, G-v 100
3. genius of the place. G-vi 320
genius of the place. G-vi 326
4. The lance . . . was of blue . . . G-i 164
blue lance. G-vi 719
5. With hot tears stirring in their inmost hearts. G-i 258
Then tears like rain were stirred within their hearts, G-ii 267
6. the sun-born maid G-iv 807
the sun-born girl G-vi 134
7. golden master [Constantine] G-iv 188
golden Constantine, G-iv 103
8. they sounded trumpets and returned at once. G-i 330
They sounded trumpets, and returned again. G-iv 827
9. All by himself he dared encounter thousands, G-iv 638
You'd not have dared to march alone on thousands. G-iv 697
10. So, drawing swords, they thrust within arm's length, G-i 178
But drew my sword, and came within arm's length. G-vi 703
11. Ambron's grandson; nephew of Karoës. G-i 285
Ambron his grandsire, Karöes his uncle. G-iv 37
12. He ran through Charziané to Cappadocia, G-i 56
And plundered Charziané and Cappadocia. G-iv 42
13. Fastened his skirts up firmly to his belt, G-iv 116
Fastened his skirts up firmly to his belt, G-iv 1058
14. And do not think you'll suffer hurt from us, G-iv 699
And don't suspect you'll suffer hurt from us. G-iv 986
15. I'll make your marriage known throughout the world, G-iv 704
I'll make your marriage known throughout the world. G-iv 724
16. Have sworn with the most awe-inspiring oaths, G-i 111
Their generals vowed with awe-inspiring oaths G-ii 67
and swore to me with awe-inspiring oaths. G-v 85
17. And why deny your kin, your faith and country, G-ii 54
I have denied my faith and kin for you. G-ii 190
Forget his kin, his parents and his country, G-iii 11
18. A countless host on foot came out to meet them. G-iv 877
An endless crowd of women came to meet them. G-iv 842
19. Great crowds of relatives came out to meet them, G-ii 30

[xxxi]

Great was the crowd of relatives and friends G-ii 297
20. And gave three thousand chosen lancers to me.
I quelled all Syria and captured Kufah   G-i 291-92
They gave three thousand chosen lancers to him;
He quelled all Syria and captured Kufah,   G-iv 38-39

These are only a few of a large number of formulas used in the Grottaferrata version, but they give the reader an idea of the material used by illiterate poets who composed poems orally.

For a fuller discussion of oral poetry, the reader is referred to Albert Lord's *The Singer of Tales*, Cambridge: Harvard University Press, 1960, and to Gareth Morgan's "Cretan Poetry: Sources and Inspiration," *Kretika Chronika*, vol. 14, part 1, 1960, Herakleion, Crete.

Oral Tradition: Rhythm and Meter. The dampening influence of the literary tradition on a poem that has been composed by the oral method can easily be seen by comparing a purely literary poem, such as Milton's translation of Psalm LXXXI with an old ballad composed in the oral tradition, such as *Sir Patrick Spens.* We can then take a few lines from *Digenis Akritas* that seem to have the dead hand of literature attached to them, and compare them with a folk song such as *Constantine and Arete.* But before beginning, it is advisable to be familiar with the principles of versification as outlined in some basic text on poetry. There are no better discussions than C. W. Lewis's *The Principles of English Verse*, New York: Henry Holt and Company, 1906 and R. M. Alden's *An Introduction to Poetry*, New York: Henry Holt and Company, 1909, if they can be found.

The first problem that arises is that of finding a suitable way to symbolize in print the subtleties of rhythm, stress, time and pitch which occur in speech. There are three methods in general use: (1) the macron and breve (— and ◡) customarily used to show long and short quantities in classical meters; (2) acute accent marks (′) over the syllables to be stressed, sometimes with secondary stresses added (″); (3) musical notation without any indication of pitch. Each system has advantages and drawbacks: the macron and breve show quantities, but stress does not always coincide with a long syllable; accent marks do not show quantities, which are more important in both English and medieval Greek than most people realize; and musical notation implies a much more rigid rhythm than actually occurs in speech, and dynamic indications are crude in comparison with the real accentuations of the living language. Nevertheless, with the full realization that musical notation is arbitrary and imprecise, we shall use it because oral poetry is composed to be sung, or at least intoned.

The next question that arises is this: what time symbol should we use to indicate the iambic rhythm of our examples? Sidney Lanier and W. Thomson say that English blank verse is written in three-eight time. T. S. Omond, although not using musical notation, believes the iambic measure is in duple, rather than in triple time. These two terms can be easily understood if we keep in mind that a horse trots in duple time, but canters in triple time; and that a march is in duple time, but a waltz in triple time. One way to find the correct musical time for iambics is to see what musicians have chosen for setting them to music, for in spite of the vast difference between the rhythm of speech and song, there must be something that leads a musician to choose the time for his music. Besides, we are studying poetry that was once sung. Because more hymns have been written in the ballad meter (known to hymn writers as C. M., or common meter) than in any other meter, we can get some help by examining all the hymns in a hymn book written in common meter.

In one hymn book, *Hymns of the Spirit,* Boston: Beacon Press, 1937, about two and a half times as many hymns have been written in duple times as in triple time. But then a few hymns have been set to two tunes, one in duple and the other in triple time. Furthermore, an examination of English and Scottish popular ballads, even without accompanying music, will show that the situation with the ballads is exactly the opposite. Most of them are in triple time. The explanation is simple. Six-eight time can be used to represent both duple and triple time, depending on the arrangement and values of the notes. If six eighth notes are combined into three quarter notes, the result is triple time, although it should probably be written as three-four time. But if these same eighth notes are combined into four dotted quarter notes, the result is the rhythm of duple time, and might be written as four-four time. In addition, there are other arrangements that will give the sensation of either duple or triple time. We must feel the sensation of either two or three beats, a judgment that is entirely subjective and therefore difficult to describe. The sensation of triple time may come on the first, second, or third beat. When six beats occur, as they do in six-eight time, it is either duple or triple time, depending on how the stresses fall. If they fall on the first, fourth, sixth, and the first beat of the next measure, we shall probably feel that the time is triple, but a slight dragging of the rhythm or weakness in the stresses may make us doubtful. However, if only the fifth beat is skipped, the "V for Victory" rhythm, there will be little doubt—it is triple time.

With these thoughts in mind, and remembering that rhythm is very subjective, let us look at some examples.

1. John Milton, Translation of Psalm LXXXI, lines 1-6

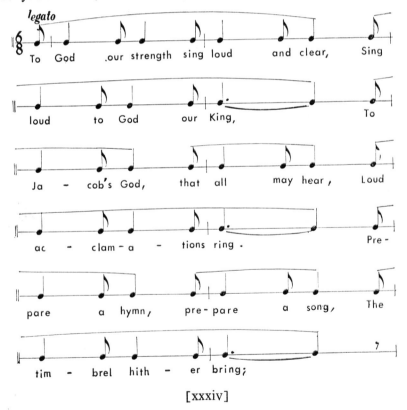

2. Sir Patrick Spens, lines 1-8

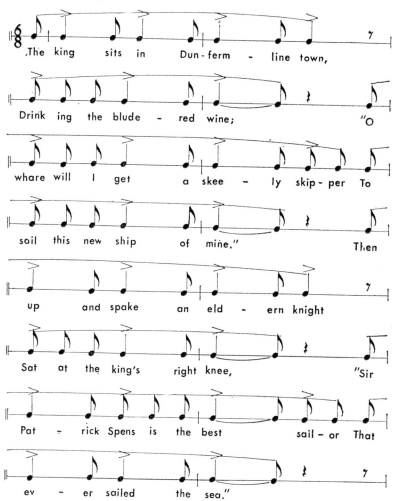

The king sits in Dun-ferm - line town,

Drink ing the blude - red wine; "O

whare will I get a skee - ly skip-per To

soil this new ship of mine." Then

up and spake an eld - ern knight

Sat at the king's right knee, "Sir

Pat - rick Spens is the best sail - or That

ev - er sailed the sea."

3. Digenis Akritas, G-iii 170-174

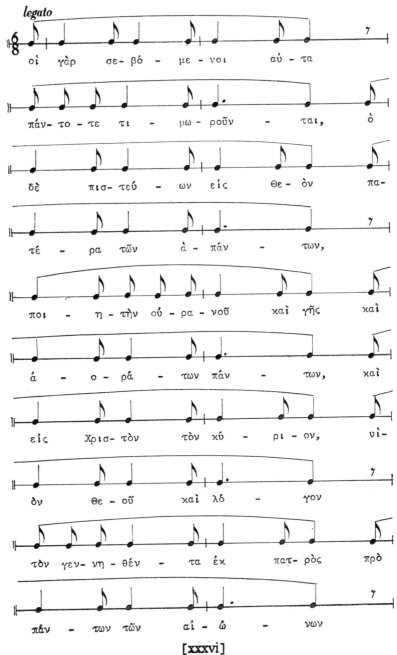

legato

οἱ γὰρ σε- βό - με - νοι αὐ - τα

πάν- το - τε τι - μω - ροῦν - ται, ὁ

δὲ πισ- τεύ - ων εἰς Θε - ὸν πα-

τέ - ρα τῶν ἁ - πάν - των,

ποι - η - τὴν οὐ - ρα - νοῦ καὶ γῆς καὶ

ἁ - ο - ρά - των πάν - των, καὶ

εἰς Χρισ- τὸν τὸν κύ - ρι - ον, υἱ-

ὸν Θε - οῦ καὶ λό - γον

τὸν γεν- νη - θέν - τα ἐκ πατ- ρὸς πρὸ

πάν - των τῶν αἰ - ώ - νων

4. Constantine and Arete

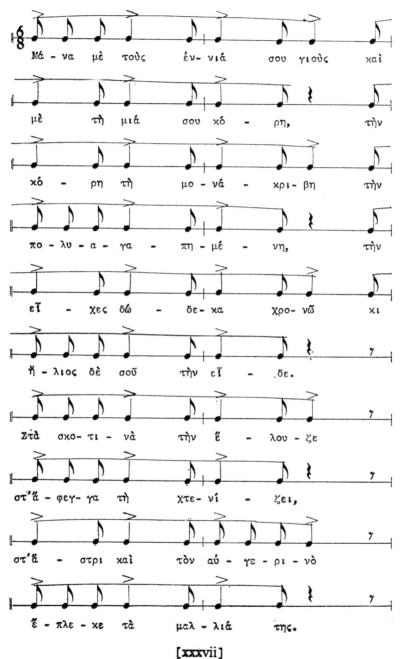

Μά - να μὲ τοὺς ἐν- νιά σου γιοὺς καὶ

μὲ τὴ μιά σου κό - ρη, τὴν

κό - ρη τὴ μο - νά - κρι- βη τὴν

πο - λυ - α - γα - πη - μέ - νη, τὴν

εἶ - χες δώ - δε- κα χρο- νῶ κι

ἥ - λιος δὲ σοῦ τὴν εἶ - .δε.

Στὰ σκο- τι - νὰ τὴν ἔ - λου - ζε

στ'ἄ - φεγ- γα τὴ χτε- νί - ζει,

στ'ἄ - στρι καὶ τὸν αὐ - γε - ρι - νὸ

ἔ - πλε - κε τὰ μαλ - λιά της.

Each line of the Greek examples has been divided and written in two lines here, partly for typographical reasons, and partly in order that it may be compared with the English on the same basis.

It will be seen at once that Milton's Psalm is slow in rhythm, not strongly marked in accents, and might almost better have been written in four-four time. The lines from *Digenis Akritas* are in triple time, move faster, and have sharper accents. The lines from *Sir Patrick Spens* and from *Constantine and Arete* are lively, brightly accented, and run along with fire and zip. One can reach the conclusion that there is more sense of movement in lines derived from the oral tradition, and that the lines here given from *Digenis Akritas* have been reworked by some well-meaning but inartistic scribe.

It needs only to be added that there are many other rhythms to be found in ballads and folk songs than the English ballad meter and the political verse, but the principle is the same: where there is oral tradition there is fire and life; where the literary tradition has been added later the fire has gone out.

Historical Counterparts. Characters in the story who seem possibly to have been historical characters are as follows:

AMBRON: Evidently Amr ibn Ubayd Allah, emir of Melitene from 835 to 863, known also as Omar. He was the son of Ubayd Allah al-Aqta, and the grandfather of Abu Hafs, both emirs of Melitene. His career overlaps the reigns of the emperors Theophilus (829-844) and Michael III (842-867), and of the caliphs al-Mutasim (833-842), al-Wathiq (842-847) and Mutawakkil (847-861).

A raid by Amr was the only military episode on the eastern frontier during the early part of Mutasim's reign. Then, in 836 the caliph sent his army against Amorium, dividing it into two parts, one under the command of Ashinas, whom Amr joined, and the other under Afshin. The two parts joined forces on the left bank of the Halys River, and besieged Amorium, the birthplace of Theophilus's father, Michael II. After stiff resistance for thirteen days, the city was betrayed and surrendered. A large number of the inhabitants were massacred, and forty-two notables were taken prisoner and executed seven years later.

For several years after this there was little military activity on the eastern front excepting the annual raids made by Amr of Melitene and Ali of Tarsus. One expedition by Amr in 844 reached Malagina, where he defeated Theoctistus, Logothete of the Drome, and one by Ali in 853 which almost reached Constantinople. During this period the Paulician heretics took refuge in Arab territory, establishing head-quarters at Tephrike, and joined forces with Amr.

In 856 Petronas, General of the Thrakesian Theme, acting in the name of the young emperor, Michael III, advanced to the Euphrates, rav-aged Paulician territory around Tephrike, and penetrated as far as Amida without resistance from either Karbeas, the Paulician leader, or Amr. In 859 Michael himself led an army to the Euphrates. Then in the summer of 860 Amr led an expedition to Sinope.

But in 863, after advancing to the Black Sea and Amisus, Amr was met on his return by the troops of Petronas near the Halys River, possibly at Malakopia, was surrounded, and when he attempted to escape, was killed.

ANNA: The name of Antakinos's wife does not occur in G, where she is simply called the General's Wife. In A 30 she is given the name Anna, a Ducas, of the family of Constantine. This is sufficiently vague to make it impossible to identify her. Theophilus had a daugh-ter named Anna and a son named Constantine. But Constantine Ducas had a son named Constantine and a daughter named Anna. The name probably was chosen because it was well known, although it can not be identified with any specific individual.

ANTAKINOS: Probably Andronicus Ducas who distinguished to join Himerius, Admiral of the Byzantine Navy, in an expedition himself by defeating the Arabs at Germanicea in 904. He was ordered against the Arabs, but was persuaded by the eunuch Samonas, a favorite of the Emperor Leo VI (although an Arab by birth and ap-parently by sympathy too) that if he embarked with Himerius he would be imprisoned and blinded. He therefore refused, and was ac-cused of treason. He first took refuge in Kavalla where he was be-sieged by loyalist troops. Then, after calling on the Arabs for help, he fled to Baghdad in 906. His defection caused the dismissal of the Patriarch Nicholas Mysticus, who was accused of entering into secret communication with him.

The name Antakinos is explained in the Turkish epic, *Saïd Battal*, in which there is a Greek general named Antaki Kafir, the Infidel from Antioch. There is no known connection between Antioch and Andronicus Ducas; however, he is called a Ducas, and in A and T his name is given as Aaron in Syrian, or Andronicus in Greek. In all versions he is called a member of the Kinnamades family. This family has not been traced, but it has been suggested that they were Armenian.

CHRYSOVERGES: Probably can be identified with Chrysocheir, leader of the Paulicians after the death of his uncle, Karbeas, in 863, who in the poem, is his brother-in-law. He led an expedition to Nicomedia and Nicaea, and after taking Ephesus, turned the church of St. John into a stable. This raid impelled Basil I to march on Tephrike, but Chrysocheir counterattacked and took Ancyra. In 872 Basil sent the Domestic of the Schools against the Paulicians, and with the help of an earthquake he razed Tephrike, took several other towns including Taranda, captured Chrysocheir, beheaded him, and sent his head back to the emperor in Constantinople. It is also possible that due to similarity of names, the redactor of the poem used the name of Nicholas II Chrysoverges, Patriarch of Constantinople (979-991).

CONSTANTINE: The brother who fought the Emir in single combat was named Constantine, and has sometimes been identified with Constantine Ducas, son of Andronicus Ducas (Antakinos above), Domestic of the Schools. During the brief reign of Alexander, following the death of Leo VI, Nicholas Mysticus, the Patriarch, called in Constantine Ducas to save the city from the Bulgars, who in 913 were threatening. Constantine attempted to take advantage of the situation by seizing the throne and was killed.

THE EMIR: A clue to the identification of this name is to be found in a muddled passage starting at E 505. The Emir, to encourage his men during the difficult trip to Syria to see his mother, reminds them of the battle of Malakopia (of which he is reminded by his mother in other versions), and says, "And I, my boys, was hunting with five brave young men: the son of Mousis; Apo Halpes, grandson of old Maiakes; and three other soldiers." By comparison with the other versions we can see that the redactor has confused the Emir with his own son, Basil, on his first hunt. But the point is that the name Apo Halpes must surely be Abu Hafs, emir of Melitene, and grandson of Amr. In 928 Abu Hafs concluded a treaty by which he agreed to bring all his troops (said to be 12,000 horsemen) over to the Byzantines. It is historical fact that nearly all these troops not only settled in Byzantine territory, but were converted to Christianity. Sources for this episode are given by *Kal.* as follows: A. Vasiliev, *Byzantines and Arabs during the Years of the Macedonian Dynasty*, (Petrograd, 1902), p. 236; Henri Gregoire, in *Byzantion*, (Paris and Brussels, 1912) 6:497; 7:288-89, 318. For more see *Kal.*, 1:1175n.

Neither Mousis nor Maiakes are explained. Mousis may be another form of Mousour; the text of E gives two others, Mousouros and Mousouphris. Maiakes, who should be Amr, is not identified.

EUDOCIA: Basil's wife is not named in G, but is called Eudocia in A and T. Eudocia Ingerina was mistress to Michael III until he married Eudocia Decapolita. After his death Eudocia Ingerina married Basil I.

IRENE: The name of the General's daughter abducted by the Emir is not given in G; in A she is called Irene. The most famous Irene was the wife of Leo IV who was sole empress from his death in 797 until 802. Although the name became common in the empire later, the only other person with whom she might have been identified is Irene Ducas, the wife of Alexius Comnenus (1081-1118) and mother of Anna Comnena, author of her father's biography, the *Alexiad*. The name, too, may have been used because of the peace-making activities attributed to her in G-vii 198 ff.

KAROËS: A name generally identified with Karbeas, leader of the Paulicians who in 856 took refuge with the Arabs in the territory around Tephrike and joined forces with Amr, emir of Melitene. Karbeas was killed in 863 during Michael's campaign against the Paulicians, and was possibly with Amr at Malakopia at the time. There is no indication in history that he was related to Amr in any way. The name has also been identified with Karghuyeh, the Chamberlain of Aleppo, whose Greek name was Karoës. Karghuyeh was defeated by Peter Phocas in December-January 969-970, and signed a treaty of allegiance with the Byzantines.

In G-ii 75, but nowhere else, the name Karoës is prefixed by the name or word Mourses which Mavrogordato capitalizes, but Kelonaros does not. Without seeing the manuscript I cannot judge whether this is a proper name or not. If it is a proper name, it may be a corruption of Mousour. But if not, it is difficult to say what it means.

MELEMENTZES: There seem to have been two Armenian soldiers of distinction named Mleh, Melias or Malih al-Armani. The first built the fortress of Tzamandus and became General of the new theme of Lycandus at the end of the reign of Leo VI in 912. The second was appointed Domestic of the East under John Tzimisces in 972, and was defeated in a battle with Abu Taghlib near Amida, when he was wounded, taken prisoner, and in 974 died of his wounds. The second Mleh is probably the counterpart of Melementzes. The name Melementzes has persisted in the form Melementzoglu, of sons of Melemenji nomad tribes in the Anti-Taurus mountains. See *Kal.*, vol. 1: A-3400 n.

MOUSELOM: There are five possible counterparts: three Armenians and two Greeks. Mushel Manikonia, an Armenian, was Viceroy to the Emperor Constans in 645; another Mushel Mamikonian was head of the anti-Arab faction in Armenia in 748; and Mushel II was King of Kars in 961. None of these is plausible. The two Greeks are: Alexius Musele, General of the Armeniakon Theme, who was blinded by his own troops at the order of the Emperor Constantine VI (780-97); and Alexius Musele, son-in-law of the Emperor Theophilus, who was sent to help in the defense of Sicily in 837, and was recalled in 844. Only the latter seems a possible counterpart.

MOUSOURS: Refers to three different persons in the poem: a highway robber G-v 168; the uncle of the Emir (A 656), where he is specifically called the Tarsite; and the Emir himself (A 302). The name is surely a corruption of the Arabic *mansur*, which means victorious, and was used by many Arabs such as al-Mansur, caliph of Baghdad (754-75), and al-Mansur, Fatimid caliph (946-953); as well as Christians such as the author of *Barlaam and Ioasaph*, St. John Damascene (c. 750) whose family name was Mansur. There can be no significance in the robber's name, but Mousour Tarsites (A 656) can hardly be anyone except Ali ibn Yahya, emir of Tarsus and later governor of Armenia. As to the Emir himself, the name is simply complimentary.

PANTHIA: The daughter of Ambron in the poem, but we have no information as to whether Amr had any daughters, and if he did, whether one was named Panthia, or, as she is named in other versions, Spathia. The name may have been borrowed: the mother of Leucippe in Achilles Tatius' *Leucippe and Cleitophon* is named Panthia; so is the mother of Hysmine in Eustathius' *Hysmine and Hysminias;* and so is the wife of Stratocles in Theodore Prodomos' *Rhodanthe.* The name Spathia may easily be a corruption of Panthia.

PHILOPAPPOS: The name is borrowed from that of the last king of the ancient kingdom of Commagene. Many legends surround this name, some of which have been woven into the poem.

Other names cannot be identified. They have been borrowed from the Hellenistic romances.

Genealogy. The two following genealogical charts show that there is a core of history in the poem, but that the poem essentially is not history, but legend. Let us begin with Basil's genealogy as given in the G version using names from the A version where none are given. For the sake of simplicity I have omitted brothers and others whose existence proves nothing.

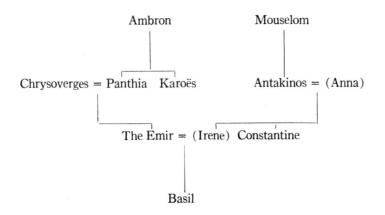

We can substitute names from the list of historical counterparts, and check these against the chronology. Discrepancies appear. Alexius Musele would have been too old to be Andronicus Ducas's father, and his family name is wrong. Perhaps he should be pushed back a generation and shown as Andronicus Ducas's maternal grandfather. Chrysocheir was actually the nephew and son-in-law of Karbeas, not his brother-in-law. Karbeas also can be pushed back a generation, and shown as Panthia's uncle. A chart to show these relationships follows:

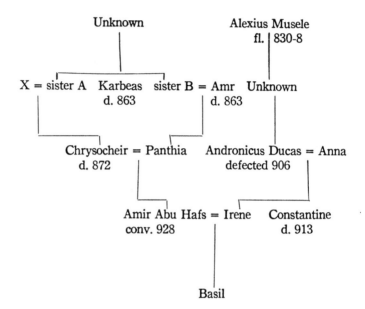

But, Constantine could not have been killed fifteen years before the conversion of the Emir; both events occurred the same year. As is common in the history of literature, the author has drawn from history for the purpose of giving life and a sense of realism to his story without concerning himself with historical accuracy.

Chronology. To assist the reader fictional names, in italics, are given with their historical counterparts, together with the names of emperors, caliphs and events, with location in the texts in parentheses, of significance in understanding the poem's relation to history. Dates are by year only.

829 Theophilus becomes emperor.
831 The Arabs take *Palermo* (G-i 101).
833 al-Mutasim becomes caliph.

835 Amr ibn Ubayd Allah (*Ambron*, G-i 285), also known as Omar, becomes emir of Melitene.

836 Theophilus takes Melitene, Sozopetra and Arsamosata.

837 In revenge al-Mutasim besieges and takes *Amorium* (G-i 8), birthplace of Theophilus' father. Amr (*Ambron*) participates in this action.

— Alexius Musele (*Mouselom*, E 146), Theophilus' son-in-law, is sent to help in the defense of Sicily.

— Military district of Charsianon (*Charzianè*, G-i 6) is formed.

— Leo the Mathematician builds the golden plane tree with the *mechanical singing birds* (A 101-10) in the Magnaura Palace for Theophilus.

842 Michael III becomes emperor.

— al-Wathiq becomes caliph.

844 Alexius Musele (*Mouselom*) is recalled from Sicily.

— Amr (*Ambron*) raids Bithynia and reaches the imperial stud farm at Malagina.

847 al-Mutawakkil becomes caliph.

853 Ali ibn Yahya, emir of Tarsus (*Mousour Tarsites*, A 656), reaches Chrysopolis across Bosporus from Constantinople in a raid.

— About this time the Paulician heretics join forces with the Arabs, and settle in the neighborhood of *Tephrike* (G-ii 78).

855 Michael's mother, the dowager Empress Theodora, separates him from his mistress, *Eudocia* Ingerina (A 1668), who later marries the Emperor Basil I, in order to marry him to *Eudocia* Decapolita.

856 The imperial army, led by Theodora's brother, Petronas, General of the Thrakesian Theme, crosses the *Euphrates* (G-iv 994) for the first time in many years, and advances as far as *Amida* (G-viii 7).

859 The Emperor Michael III himself is perhaps in command of the same army when it again crosses the *Euphrates*.

861 al-Muntasir becomes caliph.

862 al-Mustain becomes caliph.

863 Karbeas (*Karoës*, G-i 285), leader of the Paulician heretics, is **killed.**

— Amr (*Ambron*), while returning from a raid on Amisus and the Black Sea coast, is surrounded and killed by Petronas's troops at a point south of the Halys River near Malakopia (*Mellokopia*, G-iii 67).

— Ali ibn Yahya (*Mousour Tarsites*), now Governor of Armenia, is killed defending Mayyafariqin (*Meferkéh*, G-v 66).

866 al-Mutazz becomes caliph.

867 Basil I the Macedonian becomes emperor.

869 al-Muhtadi becomes caliph.

870 al-Mutamid becomes caliph.

— Chrysocheir (*Chrysoverges*, G-i 284) advances to Nicomedia and Nicaea, and raids Ephesus, where he turns the church of St. John into a stable.

872 The Emperor Basil I sends his son-in-law, Christopher, Domestic of the Schools, against the Paulicians. With the help of an earthquake he razes *Tephrike* (G-ii 78), captures Chrysocheir (*Chrysoverges*), beheads him, and sends the head back to the Emperor in Constantinople.

873 The Emperor Basil I takes Sozopetra, Samosata and other towns along the *Euphrates,* but fails to take Melitene.

882 Yazman, emir of Tarsus (*Mourses Karoës*, G-ii 75), defeats the Greeks before Tarsus.

886 Leo VI becomes emperor.

900 Leo marries a third wife, *Eudocia* Baiana (A 1668).

904 Andronicus Ducas (*Antakinos*, G-iv 54; *Aaron-Andronicus*, A 23) wins a substantial victory at Germanicea. In the belief that he would be blinded if he joined Admiral Himerius, he defects to the Arabs in 906.

912 Alexander.

— Melias, Mleh, or Malih al-Armani (*Melementzes* [?], G-vi 427) a distinguished Armenian soldier, is made the first general of the new theme of Lycandus.

913 Constantine attempts to seize the throne but is killed.

— Constantine VII Porphyrogenitus becomes emperor.

920 Romanus I Lecapenus becomes co-emperor.

928 Abu Hafs, emir of Melitene (*The Emir*, G-i 30; *Apo Halpes*, E 505), the grandson of Amr (*Ambron*), surrenders to John

Kourkouas, bringing with him 12,000 horsemen to join forces with the Byzantines. Nearly all of these troops are converted to Christianity.

934 Kourkouas captures Melitene.

944 *The Sacred Towel* (G-iii 150) is taken to Constantinople from Edessa.

— Romanus I is deposed; Constantine VII remains as sole emperor.

955 Nicephoras Phocas, appointed Domestic, intensifies the war against the Arabs.

959 Romanus II becomes emperor.

961 Mushel II (*Mouselom*[?], E 146) becomes King of Kars.

963 Nicephoras II Phocas becomes emperor.

969 John I Tzimisces becomes emperor.

— Karguyeh, Chamberlain of Aleppo, whose Greek name was *Karoës,* signs a treaty making Aleppo a Byzantine protectorate.

972 Melias (*Melementzes*), another Armenian general of the same name, is appointed Domestic of the East by John Tzimisces, is defeated by Abu Taghlib (*Haplorrabdes,* G-v 67) near *Amida,* taken prisoner, and dies of his wounds.

— Abu Taghlib (*Haplorrabdes*), emir of Mosul, pays tribute to John Tzimisces after Nisibis falls.

976 Basil II the Bulgar-slayer becomes emperor.

Excepting the final capture of Edessa by George Maniakes in 1032, there were few military campaigns between 1001 and 1056, so that it is reasonable to think that this period was called an era of peace.

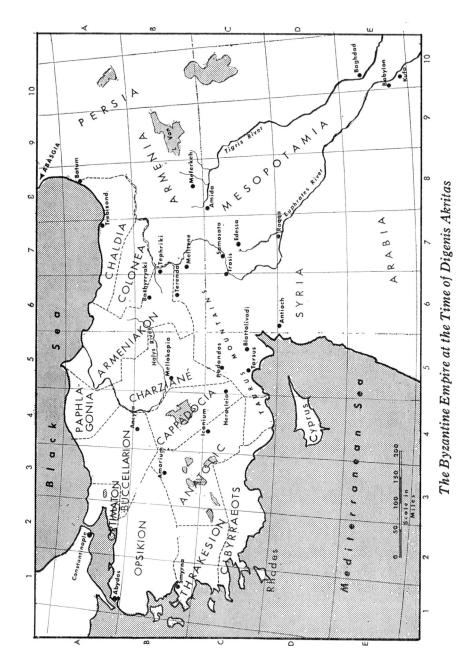

The Byzantine Empire at the Time of Digenis Akritas

Digenis Akritas

THE TWO-BLOOD BORDER LORD

The Grottaferrata Version

[*Digenis Akritas*]
[THE TWO-BLOOD BORDER LORD]

FIRST BOOK

1] [*Proem*]

Praises, trophies and an ode
To thrice-blest Basil, the Border Lord,
A man most noble and most brave,
Whose strength was a gift to him from God.
He overcame all Syria, 5
Babylon and all Charziané,
Armenia and Cappadocia,
Amorium and Iconium,
And that great famous castle too,
Though mighty and well fortified, 10
I mean Ancyra—all of Smyrna,
And conquered lands beside the sea.
Now I'll disclose to you the deeds
Which he accomplished in this life:
How he filled valiant fighting men 15
As well as all the beasts with awe,
Having as help the grace of God,
God's Mother, the indomitable,
The angels and archangels too,
And the victorious great martyrs, 20
Both the all-glorious Theodores,

*Lines are numbered according to the Greek text of Mavrogordato's *Digenes Akrites* (Oxford, 1956), or, in the case of excerpts from other versions, in accordance with the texts of Kalonaros' *Basileios Digenis Akritas* (Athens, 1941).

[3]

The army leader and recruit,
And noble George of many labors,
The miracle-working martyrs' martyr,
Sublime Demetrius, the patron   25
Of Basil, and the boast and pride
Of him who vanquished all his foes,
The Hagarenes and Ishmaelites
And barbarous Scyths who rage like dogs.

(E 1)

2] [*How a Lovely Woman Conquered the Emir*]
[*An Emir abducts the General's Daughter, is pursued by her
brothers, and defeated by the youngest in single combat. He
begs them to accept him as her future husband, and becomes
a Roman and a Christian.*]

G-i

Among the nobles was a rich emir   30
Who had both prudence and the highest courage.
He was not black like Ethiops, but fair,
Just blooming with a comely, curly beard.
His eyebrows were so ripe that they were tangled;
A quick, gay glance filled full of amorous love   35
Sprang from his countenance just like a rose.
He had the stature of a lovely cypress,
And looked, if you observed him, like a picture.
    He also had unconquerable might,
And passed his leisure fighting beasts each day   40
To test his nerve, for he admired valor.
To all he was a marvel to behold,
And to the young his fame a fearful thing.
    So, well prepared by wealth and massive courage,
He started to enlist Turks, Dilemites,   45
A few picked Arabs, Troglodytes for foot,
And had a thousand knights for his Companions,
All on his muster suitably rewarded.
    With wrath he burst out on Romania,
And, taking parts of the land of Heracles,   50

He laid waste many cities, made them desert,
Capturing countless multitudes of people
Because those places had been left unguarded,
Those guarding them then being on the border.
And therefore meeting little opposition   55
He ran through Charziané to Cappadocia,
And fell suddenly on the General's house.
  But who can tell what deeds were done in it?
None, for he slew all those discovered there,
Carried away much wealth and sacked the house,   60
Taking as prisoner a lovely girl,
A virgin still; she was the General's daughter.
The General was in exile at the time,
The maiden's brothers then were on the border.
Her mother, fleeing from the pagans' hands,   65
Forthwith wrote to her sons all that had happened,
The pagans' coming and the maiden's capture,
The parting from her dear, her many woes,
And to her letter added this with tears:
  "O most belovéd children, pity your mother,   70
A most unhappy soul about to die.
Be mindful of your love for your own sister;
So free your sister and your mother quickly,
Her from harsh slavery, and me from death.
We'd give our very soul for our dear daughter,   75
So, for your sister's sake, don't heed your lives.
Have pity, children mine, on your own sister;
Bestir yourselves, and hurry to her rescue.
You'll see a mother dying for her child,
And you'll be cursed by me and by your father   80
If you don't do exactly what I've told you."
  Now when they heard these words they sighed deeply,
And when all five had become drenched with tears,
They urged each other to depart quickly,
Saying, "Let us begone and die for her!"   85
  They mounted and went on their way again
With a few soldiers following along.

Sparing no pains, with sleeping never sated,
In a few days they came to the encampment
In that dread pass which is called Difficult. 90
There they dismounted far off from the outposts,
And, at their own suggestion in a note,
Were brought to the Emir by his command.
  He was seated upon his lofty throne,
A dread gold-inlaid thing outside his tent, 95
With armed men standing around him in a circle.
When they were near, he listened to their stories.
So, kneeling on each step up to the third,
They spoke these words to the Emir with tears:
  "Emir, servant of God and Syria's prince, 100
May you go to Palermo, see the Mosque,
May you, Emir, kneel to the Hanging Stone,
And be found fit to kiss the Prophet's Tomb,
And may you listen to the sacred prayer.
You've carried off a charming girl, our sister. 105
Sell her to us, servant of the All-highest;
We'll give for her whatever wealth you bid.
Her father grieves for her, his only daughter;
Her mother, now she's vanished, wants to die;
And we, who have a boundless feeling for her, 110
Have sworn with the most awe-inspiring oaths,
To bring her back again, or all be slain."
  Hearing this, the Emir admired their daring,
But to find out if they were really brave
(He knew, you see, the Roman tongue precisely), 115
He answered very gently, saying this:
  "If you desire to set your sister free,
Choose one among you who you think is noble,
And let us mount our horses, he and I,
And fight in single combat, he and I. 120
Then, if I win, I'll keep you for my slaves,
But, if he wins, then without argument,
You'll get your sister, with no retribution,
As well as other captives here with me.

[6]

For otherwise I will not yield your sister   125
Even if you give me all Romania's wealth.
So go! Consider what is best for you!"
    Straightway they all withdrew, cheered up by hope,
But lest they quarrel over who should fight,
Decided to cast lots and end contention.   130
The lot fell to the young one, Constantine,
The latest born, who was his sister's twin.
The eldest, while preparing him, advised him,
And said, "Don't let the shouting scare you, brother;
Don't be afraid, nor let the blows appall.   135
And, if you see a naked sword, don't run,
Nor flee from anything more terrible.
In face of your mother's curse, don't spare your youth.
Supported by her prayers, you'll beat your foe,
For God will not permit us to be slaves.   140
Go, son! Cheer up! And have no fear at all!"
And facing toward the east, they called on God:
"Do not allow us, Lord, to be enslaved!"
Embracing him, they sent him forth, and said:
"So may our parents' prayer be your right hand!"   145
    He mounted on his horse, a well-bred black,
And girding on his sword, he took his lance,
And hung his mace beside him on its baldric.
Secured on all sides by the sign of the cross,
He spurred his horse, and rode out to the field.   150
    He toyed first with his sword and then his lance,
And certain Saracens sneered at the youth:
"See what they've sent to fight in single combat
With him whose Syrian triumphs were so great!"
One Saracen, a Dilemite border lord,   155
Quietly spoke these words to the Emir:
"You see how cleverly he uses spurs,
And parries with his sword and twirls his lance.
These things denote experience and courage.
Watch you don't meet the young man carelessly!"   160
    Out came the Emir, mounted upon his charger,

Most arrogant and fearsome to the sight.
His armor glittered in the shafts of sunlight,
The lance he wielded was of blue and gold;
And all came out at once to watch the battle.   165
His horse played charmingly, amazing all,
For, gathering four feet into one place,
It balanced as if held by some device.
At other times its trot appeared so light
It seemed to skim, rather than walk, the ground.   170
And the Emir was pleased so much he smiled,
Then spurred his horse and rode out to the field,
A screaming eagle and a hissing snake,
A lion roaring to devour the youth.
At once the youth received him with dispatch,   175
And both struck with their lances which both broke,
For neither had the strength to unseat the other.
So, drawing swords, they thrust within arm's length,
And cut each other up for many hours.
The mountains echoed, hills kept thundering,   180
And blood was flowing over all the ground
While horses panicked, seized by consternation.
Though both were wounded, neither one was winning.
The Saracens, seeing the unforeseen,
And marveling at the young man's eagerness,   185
His stiff resistance and his noble daring,
All called, as with one voice, to the Emir:
"Ask for a truce! And put aside the fighting!
The Roman's dangerous; don't let him hurt you!"
Then in an instant the Emir took flight,   190
The boaster beaten by the force of might—
For boasting really isn't good at all!
He threw his sword away, held his hands high,
And crossed his fingers as their custom is,
And to the boy he raised his voice and cried: 195
"Have done, young man! The victory is yours!
Here! Take your sister and the prisoners!"
Ending the show, they went off to his tent,

And one could see the brothers filled with joy.
  With hands held high, they glorified the Lord: 200
"The glory, God, is Thine alone," they said,
"For he who trusts in Thee shall not be shamed."
They embraced their brother with the utmost joy;
Some kissed his hands, and others kissed his head,
But all entreated the Emir with warmth: 205
"Give us, Emir, our sister as you promised;
Give comfort to the heart weighed down with grief."
  Said the Emir to them, not being truthful:
"Here, take my signet ring. Go around the tents;
Search everywhere, look at the whole encampment,   210
And when you find her, take her and get out!"
  They took the signet ring with great delight,
And searched with care, not knowing the deceit.
When they'd been all around and had found nothing,
They came straight back to the Emir, grieving.   215
En route they met a rustic Saracen
Who said to them through their interpreter:
"Whom are you seeking, boys, and whom lamenting?"
And, still lamenting, they replied in turn:
"You've taken prisoner a maid, our sister;   220
We cannot find her, so we want to die!"
  The Saracen, however, sighed and said:
"Go to the lower gorge; you'll find a brook
Where yesterday we slaughtered many beauties
Because they would not do what they were told."   225
  They spurred their horses, went off to the brook,
And found the slaughtered women dyed in blood,
Some lacking hands, and others heads or feet,
Some all their limbs, and some with entrails out,
Impossible to recognize at all.   230
  And when they saw these things they were dismayed,
And picking up dust, poured it on their heads.
And moved to tears deep in their hearts, they cried:
"Which hand shall we bewail, which head lament?
Bring which limb, when we know it, to our mother?   235

[9]

O sister, why were you unjustly slain?
O sweetest soul, why did this happen to you?
Why set before your time, quenching our light?
Why cut up limb from limb by barbarous hand?
Why was the killer's hand not paralyzed?   240
He had no mercy on your charming youth;
He had no pity for your lovely voice.
But you, you noble soul, before corruption
You chose to die, destroyed by butchery.
But, O most lovely sister, soul and heart,   245
How shall we separate you from the others?
Shan't we have even this small consolation?
O hour of horror and deceitful day,
Would you had never seen the light of sunrise,
God filling you with darkness, since our sister   250
Was sinfully carved up by lawless men!
What message shall we bring our pitiful mother?
O sun, why did you envy our fair sister,
And slay her when she vied with you in brilliance?"
    However, as they could not find their sister,   255
They made a single grave and buried all.
Then weeping they returned to the Emir
With hot tears stirring in their inmost hearts.
    "Give us, Emir, our sister, or else slay us!
Not one of us is going home without her;   260
We'll all be slaughtered for our sister's sake!"
    Hearing and seeing them lament, the Emir
Asked them, "Whose sons and from what place are you?
And from what family? What theme do you live in?"
    "We're nobles from the Anatolic Theme,   265
Our father traces from the Kinnamades,
Our mother a Ducas, kin of Constantine.
Twelve generals are our cousins or our uncles.
From such we and our sister are descended.
Our father's exiled for some foolishness   270
Which certain swindlers caused him to be blamed for.
Not one of us was present at your coming.

[10]

Indeed, we were commanding on the borders;
For, had we been there, this would not have happened:
You never would have gone inside our house.   275
But, since we weren't, you well may boast of it.
Now, greatest of Emirs and Syria's Prince,
Kneel to Baghdad; then tell us who you are.
Then, if our kin return from their campaign,
And if they bring our father back from exile,   280
We'll track you down wherever you may be,
For we won't let your rash act go unpunished."
    "My good young men," the Emir replied, "I'm son
Of Chrysoverges and of Panthia;
Ambron's grandson; nephew of Karoës.   285
My father died while I was still an infant;
My mother gave me to my Arab kinsmen
Who brought me up a good Mohammedan.
Seeing me fortunate in all my wars,
They made me ruler of all Syria,   290
And gave three thousand chosen lancers to me.
I quelled all Syria and captured Kufah
(In telling you the truth I boast but little).
Later I wiped out Heracleia, taking
Amorium up to Iconium,   295
And subdued hordes of thieves and all the beasts.
    No generals could withstand me, and no armies;
A lovely woman, though, has conquered me.
Her beauty fires me, and her weeping quenches;
Her sighing burns; I don't know what to do!   300
On her account I wished to test your courage,
Because she never ceased to weep for you.
I will confess to you and tell the truth:
If you won't scorn me as your brother-in-law,
I will become, because she's so delightful,   305
A Christian, and come to Romania.
And, by the Prophet, know this as a fact:
She never gave me a kiss nor spoke a word.
Come to my tent; see her whom you are seeking."

[11]

When they had heard these words, with utmost joy 310
They raised the tent-flap, went inside, and found
A couch with golden spread, the maid upon it.
And as she lay there, Christ! she shone like sunlight,
Her eyes all overflowing with her tears.
Her brothers saw, and quickly raised her up, 315
And each one kissed her with astonishment.
For unexpected joy, coming unhoped for,
Makes all rejoice who had no hope of it.
They suffered all at once grief, tears and pain,
But joy, most wonderful of all, began. 320
And while they were embracing her with gladness,
They added tears to all their cries, and said:
"You are alive! Alive! O soul and heart,
We thought that you were dead, carved by the sword.
It was your beauty, dear, that saved your life, 325
For beauty makes even the robbers mild,
And foes are merciful to youth and beauty."
  So promising the Emir on oath to wed him,
If he came to Romania, to their sister,
They sounded trumpets and returned at once. 330
And all perplexed, they said to one another:
"We see a wondrous thing, the power of passion!
It breaks down prisons, and it breaks up armies,
Makes one deny his faith, and not fear death!"
  And through the whole wide world the tale was bruited 335
Of how one noble maiden with her beauty
Had broken up the famous Syrian armies.

SECOND BOOK

About the Birth of the Border Lord

[*In due course after the wedding Basil is born. The Emir's mother writes and begs him to return to Syria. He plans a secret trip, but is discovered. After explanation and a promise to return, he leaves.*]

Since they had sworn that he should wed their sister,
The Emir took his Companions, and at once
Went to Romania for his belovéd.
And when he reached Romanian parts he freed
All of the people he had taken captive,   5
Giving each one provisions for the road.
The maiden's brothers wrote their mother how
They found their sister; of the Emir's desire;
How he denied his faith, his kin and country;
And said, "Belovéd mother, feel no sorrow,   10
For we shall have a good and handsome bridegroom.
Make ready all that's needful for the wedding."
    When she heard this, she returned thanks to God:
"Praise to Thy loving kindness, O my Christ!
And praises to Thy might, hope of the hopeless!   15
What willest canst; there's nought Thou canst not do;
For Thou hast tamed this enemy of ours,
And hast redeemed our daughter too from death,
    "But O my cherished daughter, light of my eyes,
When shall I see you alive, and hear your voice?   20
See! I've prepared what's needful for your wedding!
But—will the groom compare with you in beauty,
Or have the sentiments of noble Romans?

I fear, dear child, he will be heartless, fierce
As a pagan, and my life unbearable."   25
So sang the General's wife while she rejoiced,
    But the Emir, and with him the maid's brothers,
Gladly but wearily began the journey.
And when they were approaching their own house,
Great crowds of relatives came out to meet them,   30
And then the General's wife, arrayed in splendor.
    But who can tell the limitless delight
Which they all felt, or who can wholly match it?
The children kissed their mother with affection,
The mother kept rejoicing in her children,   35
And truly happy when she saw the bridegroom,
She offered thanks to God with all her heart:
"Lord Christ," she said, "whoever hopes in Thee
Has never failed to gain his heart's desire."
    And coming to the house, they held the wedding,   40
And sanctified the groom in holy baptism.
Delight, that universal joy, grew greater,
For the Emir rejoiced in his belovéd.
Indeed, there is no greater joy than loving;
The more the lover is inflamed by failure,   45
The more he is rejoiced in his belovéd.
After they had been joined, the girl conceived
And bore the Two-Blood, Basil the Border Lord.
Yet still the passion of the Emir increased.
    From Syria his mother sent a letter   50
Full of complaint and of reproach and blame.
"You've blinded both my eyes, put out my light,
Dear child. Oh, why did you forget your mother?
And why deny your kin, your faith and country,
And be disgraced in all of Syria?   55
To everyone we have become abhorrent,
Deniers of the faith, the law's transgressors,
People who don't observe the Prophet's word.
What happened, child, and why did you forget?
Why weren't you mindful of your father's deeds,   60

[14]

The Romans that he slew, the slaves he took,
The prisons that he filled with generals?
Did he not pillage many Roman districts,
And carry noble beauties off as captives?
Like you, was he not tempted by transgressions?   65
For when the Roman troops surrounded him,
Their generals vowed with awe-inspiring oaths
Their Emperor would make him a patrician,
Master of Horse, if he'd throw down his sword.
But he observed the Prophet's ordinances,   70
Despised the fame, and paid no heed to wealth.
They cut him limb from limb, and took his sword.

    "But you, though not coerced, disregard all,
Your faith, your kin, and even me, your mother.
My brother, Mourses Karoës, your uncle,   75
Led raids on Smyrna on the seacoast, ravaged
Ancyra, and the city of Abydos,
Tephrike, Taranda, and the Six Towns,
Conquered them, and returned to Syria.
But what a raid you've made, you ill-starred man!   80
You might have had the whole of Syria praise you,
But ruined all for the love of a swine-eater,
And have become accursed in every mosque.

    "If you don't come to Syria at once,
The emirs intend to throw me in the river,   85
Slay the children of an apostate father,
And give to other men your charming damsels,
Who, though they sigh for you, won't remain constant.

    "O my sweet child, have pity on your mother!
Don't lead my old age to the grave in sorrow,   90
Don't let your children be unjustly slain,
Don't overlook your charming damsels' tears,
And have great God uproot you from the world.
As you can see, I've sent you chosen horses:
Ride on the bay, and lead the black beside you,   95
And let the chestnut follow. Let none catch you!
Take, if you grieve for her, the Roman girl.

But, if you disregard me, then be cursed!"
   Taking her letter, picked Arabians
Came to Romania with utmost speed.   100
There was a place far off called Lakkopetra,
Where they encamped that they might not be seen.
Then, through the letter-bearer, they explained:
"It's moonlight all night; if you wish, we'll go."
   When the Emir had seen his mother's letter   105
He felt a son's compassion for his mother,
Felt pity for his children and their mothers,
And jealousy lest they have other men.
Never does one forget a former love,
Though love for the maiden had obscured this fact,   110
For the more violent pain obscures the lesser.
He stood in doubt, wanting to get things over.
   Coming to his belovéd's room, he said:
"I want to entrust you with a certain secret,
But I'm afraid, my dear, that you won't like it.   115
Look! The time has come to learn for certain
If your affection for me is unmixed."
   Now when she heard these words, her heart was stung.
With a deep sigh, she spoke such words as these:
"O sweetest husband, master and protector,   120
You've never spoken an unpleasant word.
What circumstance can change my love for you?
Even if I must die, I'll not reject you,
For circumstance can also prove affection."
"Don't think of death, my dear!" the Emir replied.   125
"Heaven forbid your planning it, sweet soul!
No; but my mother wrote from Syria
That I've endangered her. I want to go there,
And if you too, dear soul, will come with me,
I won't be parted from you for one hour,   130
And we'll return again with utmost haste."
   "With joy, my lord," the girl replied, "I'll go
Wherever you command; so do not worry."
God then performed an unexpected marvel:

[16]

He brought the secret plan to light in a dream.   135
The maiden's youngest brother saw the dream,
And rising up from sleep, he called his brothers,
And told the dream which he had seen that night.
"I was sitting above, inside the house,
While I was watching hawks on Lakkopetra.   140
A hostile falcon was pursuing a dove,
And as he followed and was catching her,
Both of the birds came flying in the chamber
Within which live our brother-in-law and sister.
I jumped up quickly, and I ran to catch her,   145
My spirits in confusion. Then I woke."
 The eldest then interpreted the dream:
"Hawks, so they say, are predatory men;
The falcon which you saw, our brother-in-law.
He might do injury to the dove, our sister.   150
So let's go up there where you saw the dream,
While you were watching while the hawks were flying."
 They took to horse at once, rode to the stone,
And there they found the Arabs with their horses.
Shocked at the sight, they marveled at the vision.   155
"Companions of our brother-in-law," they said,
"Welcome. But why pass up our house for this?"
The men, unable to deny the plot,
Confessed, disclosed the facts, concealing nothing,
For fear, when unexpected, brings out truth,   160
But when it is expected, breeds excuses.
They took them to their brother-in-law at once,
Rebuking him for being ill-advised.
The youngest, too, was still more vehement:
"You made this plan," he said, "so don't deny it!   165
Know, Saracen, you shan't see Syria!
So, since you've shown yourself a lawless foe,
Let our sister go, and disown your child,
Take what you brought, and go back where you came from!"
 When the Emir heard this, and saw they knew,   170
He couldn't answer, and kept utter silence,

[17]

For he was filled with shame and fear, and crushed;
Shamed by detection; being a stranger, fearful;
And pained to think of parting from his dearest.
Not knowing what to do, he went to the girl,   175
In her alone hoping to find some solace.
He did not know what God had shown in a dream.
   "Why did you do this?" he exclaimed with tears.
"Is this your love, and this the way you promise?
Did I not lay my wishes all before you?   180
And did you not gladly agree to come?
Did I compel you, or use violence?
Rather, you forced me to permit your coming,
Both to enjoy the trip and the return.
But with no fear of God before your eyes,   185
You've made your brothers come to murder me.
Remember what I did with you at first?
I captured you, but honored like a lady.
I wished a slave; I am your slave instead.
I have denied my faith and kin for you,   190
For love of you I came to Romania.
Now in exchange, girl, you've remembered death!
Look, dear, don't violate the vows between us;
Don't disavow the rapturous love we've had.
For if your brothers push me and compel me,   195
Be sure I'll draw my sword and kill myself,
And God will have to judge between us two.
Then may your petty nobles all rebuke you
Because you couldn't keep your husband's secret!
Delilah thus sent Samson to be slaughtered."   200
   Thus the Emir, weeping, spoke to the girl,
For he assumed that she'd revealed his plan—
Dishonored love indeed brings on reviling.
And when the girl heard this, she lost all speech,
And could not utter any words at all,   205
But remained looking downcast many hours.
The guilty one is ready with excuses;
The innocent has not a word to say.

[18]

But when at length she pulled herself together,
She said with tears, "Why do you chide me falsely?   210
And why accuse the one who loves you most?
I, heaven forbid, would not disclose your plan!
If I did that, earth swallow me alive,
And make me an example to the world
Of one who made her husband's secret known!"   215
And seeing the Emir's distress increasing,
For he was nearly crazy with affliction—
And great affliction breeds insanity,
Hence many become desperate and lawless—
She feared he'd kill himself with his own sword.   220
Tearing her hair, she ran out to her brothers:
"Sweet brothers, why, without reason, thus torment
One who has done no wrong? See! He is dying!
And see! He will destroy himself from madness!
Before God, brothers, let no guest be wronged   225
Who, for my sake, denied his faith and kin!
Indeed, he never did mean to oppose you;
But, fearing his mother's curse, he was just now
Leaving for Syria, returning with her.
He told me what he planned, and showed her letter.   230
Well, did not you, to heed our mother's curse,
Make bold to go, though few, against his thousands,
And for my sake join battle in the pass,
Not fearing death more than a mother's curse?
He also fears the same, and wants to go."   235
   The girl said to her brothers all these things,
Shedding hot tears and pulling out her hair.
They could not bear to see their sister weeping,
So, with one voice, while kissing her, they cried:
   "All of us hold you very dear at heart!   240
So, if you wish to send your husband forth,
Let him make God his witness he'll return,
And we'll all pray he'll have a prosperous journey."
   At once they all went to their brother-in-law,
And asked his pardon for the things they'd said: 245

"Brother, forget the ignorance of our words.
The sin was wholly yours, and not our fault:
You didn't tell us what you planned to do."
And so he pardoned them, and kissed them all.
Then, facing toward the east, with hands raised high,   250
He cried, "O Christ! O Son and Word of God,
Who ledst me to the light of knowing God,
Who hast redeemed me from the dark and doubt,
Who knowest the secret reasonings of the heart:
If ever I forget my dearest wife,   255
Or that sweet blossom, our belovéd child,
And do not come back quickly from my mother,
May I be food for mountain birds and beasts,
And afterwards not numbered among Christians!"
      Then he began preparing for the road,   260
And made all ready within fifteen days,
So his departure was well known to all,
And a great crowd of kin and friends assembled.
      Then one could see what love there was between them,
For the Emir held the girl by the hand,   265
And went alone with her into their chamber.
Then tears like rain were stirred within their hearts,
And sighs were heard from one and then the other:
"Give me your word, give me your ring, my lady,
And let me wear it, dear, till I return!"   270
And the girl sighed, and said to the Emir:
"My golden lord, don't overstep your vows;
God will requite you should you clasp another,
For God's a just judge who requites what's due!"
"If I do that, my dear," the Emir replied,   275
"Or break faith with the rapturous love we've had,
Or if I bruise your heart, my noblest darling,
Then may earth yawn, and may Hell swallow me—
I'd wish I'd never had your fragrant self!"
      With fond embraces and insatiate kisses   280
So that the time was very much drawn out,
They both became bedrenched with many tears,

[20]

And could not bear to part with one another,
All unashamed before the assembled crowd,
For love that's natural brings shamelessness,   285
A thing that all know who have learned to kiss.
Then taking up his child within his arms,
He wept, and cried to all in hearing distance:
"Will God not make me worthy to behold you,
My sweetest child, before me as a knight?   290
Or teach the use of the spear, my two-blood son,
So all your relatives may boast of you?"
And, seeing the Emir, they all shed tears.
    So, mounting upon swift and well-groomed horses,
The Emir's Companions rode out from the house.   295
Then came the Emir, mounted upon his charger.
Great was the crowd of relatives and friends
Who went with him up to the three mile mark
Where he embraced them all, made them turn back,
Then followed down the road with his Companions.   300

THIRD BOOK

The [Emir's] Return from Syria with his Mother too

[*The Emir goes to Syria, is reproached as an apostate by his mother, but converts her to Christianity, and brings her back to Romania with him.*]

Thus every lover is the slave of Love,
For he's a judge who tries the hearts of those
Not holding closely to the paths of love.
He shoots his arrows straight, he hits the heart,
And rises up with fire to inflame the reason.   5
He who's possessed by him cannot escape,
No matter whether very rich or famous,
For when aroused, Love quickly overtakes him.
　And so it chanced. That wonderful Emir,
Despising glory and the highest office,   10
Forgot his kin, his parents and his country,
And utterly denied his faith for love
Of a delightful, truly well-born maiden.
The one-time foe was seen to be Love's slave,
And for his love lived in Romania,   15
Received his mother's note from Syria,
And planned to leave because he feared her curse.
Indeed, it's fitting not to anger parents.
They all took counsel, and upon his oath,
They sent him forth rejoicing on his way.   20
　To calm the girl he then began a song:
"Strain every muscle, men! And shirk not, horses!
Hurry by day, and keep awake by night,
No matter if there's rain and snow and frost,
For I must not delay the appointed hour,   25
Be censured on return, and wish to die!"

[23]

And then, "Farewell, O kin and friends!" he added,
Embraced them all, and begged them all to pray;
And with one voice they did so right away:
"May gracious God prosper you on your journey, 30
And may we be vouchsafed to see you soon."
    From there they all returned to the house again,
Gloomy and downcast, for they suffered badly,
For such is parting to all those who love:
It burns the soul and it subdues the heart, 35
And separation wholly shatters reason.
    Then with haste the Emir took to the road,
And each day sent back letters to his love:
"Don't grieve for me, I beg, but pray instead."
And his Companions he implored with feeling: 40
"Leaders," he said, "Companions, friends and brothers,
For my sake keep alert and bear the toil;
For you made covenants and promises
In which you said that you would die for me.
But now the labor's not for death, but love. 45
My soul is blazing and my heart is scorched;
I know the endless distance we must go.
Friends, shall we ever cross the fearsome plains,
The dreadful mountains and the awful passes,
And look on Rachav, and behold my mother? 50
And shall we ever pass all these again,
And come to fair Romania once more?
And shall I ever see my pretty dove,
And that fair flower of mine, my handsome son?
Who will provide me wings, and spread them, dearest, 55
To give me an hour's rest within your arms?
How often will she sigh for me while wakeful,
Watching the highways for me every day?
Many an anxious thought comes to our loved ones,
And perils, fears and worries keep on growing. 60
But, O my noble youths, my good Companions,
Shake sleep and indolence aside completely,
That we may come to Castle Rachav quickly,

Be done, and go back to Romania.
You often have been snatched by me from danger,   65
And, skipping most of them, I'll mention one
Which recently occurred at Mellokopia
When generals surrounded us completely,
And armies stood around us like a wall,
And you were driven to despair of death,   70
All shut within them, just as in a tomb,
Without hope any of you could escape.
But I spurred forward, drove into their midst,
And sent to Hell—indeed, you know how many,
Making them flee, and beating them alone,   75
So we were saved unhurt with all our captives;
Right now there is no war; our task is love;
And in this task I beg you'll be my helpers."
  This, and much else, said the Emir to those
With him upon the road, with pain at heart.   80
For Love inflames those subject to him so
That they proclaim him, and despise all else.
  When his Companions heard, they said at once:
"Master, encamp in any place you wish.
You'll find in us no pretexts to be idle."   85
Then came an awsome sight, though none will doubt it,
For it was Love that helped and worked with all:
They traveled three days' journeys every day!
  And when they came to uninhabited passes,
He'd circle around, protecting his Companions.   90
While they were going through one dreadful pass,
They found a fearsome lion holding a fawn;
And when they saw this, his Companions ran
Right up the mountain, terrified, at once.
Distressed at this, the Emir said to the lion: 95
"How do you dare, you dangerous beast, to do this?
To stand and block the path of passionate love?
I'll give you the reward that you deserve!"
He struck it full in the middle with his mace,
And stretched the hateful beast upon the ground.   100

[25]

Then the Emir directed his Companions:
"Now pull out every one of the beast's teeth,
And likewise pull the claws from its right forepaw,
So when I reach Romania, God willing,
We may then put them on my handsome son,   105
The Two-Blood Cappadocian Border Lord."
Then eagerly he took the road again,
Outstripping others in his eager march.
None took it easy, none partook of sleep,
For Love made each one wish to beat the others.   110
   Now when they were approaching Castle Rachav,
He ordered them to pitch their tents outside,
And two of his Companions went inside,
So they might tell his mother of his coming.
And this they did, proceeding very quickly.   115
And when his mother heard what news they brought,
She actually danced a bit for joy.
And when his kinsmen too had been informed,
They went together, all of them, to meet him.
And while they were approaching where the tents were,   120
The Emir advanced on foot in boots to meet them.
They recognized him, and at once dismounted,
And filled with joy, eyes brimming with their tears—
For joy brings tears when it comes suddenly—
They all embraced him, and they shared their love: 125
His kinsmen kissed him here, his mother there,
His damsels too— in fact they brought their children—
Hugged him and kissed him most insatiately,
And did not want to part with him at all.
   Then, when they reached the tent, they sat right down,   130
And the Emir's mother began to speak:
"O sweetest child of mine, light of my eyes,
The comfort of my soul in my old age,
My joy and pleasure, and my heart's delight,
Why did you loiter in Romania?   135
Not seeing you, I wished to see no light,
No shining sun, nor live upon this earth.

Do miracles happen in Romania
Such as are done, child, at the Prophet's Tomb
Where you went with me when I went to prayers?   140
Did you not see a miracle one night
When, with no light, a splendor from on high
Filled the whole house with an ineffable gleam?
Did you not see bears, lions, wolves and sheep,
And many kinds of beasts feeding together,   145
None injuring another one at all,
But simply waiting till the end of prayer,
When, bending knees, they went away at once?
What greater marvel has Romania?
Do we not have with us the Towel of Naaman   150
Who was a king of the Assyrians
Thought worthy, for his virtue, of such wonders?
Why, son, did you offend against these things,
Despising office and the highest fame?
All thought that you were going to conquer Egypt,   155
But you became your own worst enemy,
And for a Roman girl spoiled everything!"
   She wanted to say other things like this,
But stopping her, the young man told his mother:
"Mother, I'm well acquainted with all this.   160
Before I shared the Light, I truly honored
Things really fit for darkness and destruction.
But when God in the highest thought it proper—
God willingly bore poverty for me,
And wished that He might always bear my burden—   165
To snatch me from the gullet of the Beast,
And thought me worthy of rebirth in water,
I quit such things as trumperies and fables
That truly would produce eternal fire.
For those who worship them are always punished,   170
But he who believes in God, Father of all things,
Maker of heaven, earth, and the unseen world;
In Christ the Lord, the Son and Word of God,
Begotten of the Father before all time,

[27]

Light from the Light, the great and one true God,   175
Who came down on the earth for us, mankind,
And Who was born of a virgin mother, Mary,
And suffered on the cross for our salvation,
Was buried in a tomb which you too honor,
And rose up from the dead on the third day,   180
Exactly as the Holy Scriptures teach us,
And sits upon the right hand of the Father,
And of Whose kingdom there shall be no end;
And in the Holy Spirit, which makes all live,
Which, with the Father, Son and Word, I worship,   185
And to remit my sins, confess baptism,
Awaiting the resurrection of the dead,
And the requital of those sinned against,
Forgiveness of the righteous as was promised,
And everlasting life in future ages.   190
All those believing in the Holy Trinity,
Baptized in the name of the eternal Father
And of his timelessly begotten Son,
And of the Holy Spirit, quickening all things,
Shall never perish, but shall live forever.   195
He who does not yet know this, sweetest mother,
Is punished in the eternal fire of Hell;
There is much weeping there and gnashing of teeth."
    Thus said the Emir, and, opening up the way
To the true faith, spoke to his mother thus: 200
"I'm going, mother, to Romania
To ratify my faith in the Trinity.
All of the world is not worth just one soul,
For, if we gain all, and we lose our soul,
There is no profit at all in that last hour   205
When God shall come from heaven to judge the world,
And summon all to settle their accounts.
Then shall we hear a Voice bidding us go
Into the outer and accurséd fire,
And to remain there with the devil forever   210
For disobedience to His commands.

But those with faith in Christ, as it is meet,
And those who've heeded His august commands,
Shall shine out as the sun does at that hour,
And they shall hear the voice of their good master: 215
'Come, all ye blest by the Father, and inherit
The kingdom of heaven I've prepared for you.'
All these shall go forth to eternal life;
The judge is just, and gives deserved rewards.
Mother, if you'd be thought worthy of life,   220
And ransomed from eternal dark and fire,
Flee from vain error and fictitious myths,
And recognize God in Three Persons, all
United in one substance unconfounded.
Believe your son, and come with me. I'll be   225
Your father in the Holy Spirit, the sponsor
In your regeneration, when baptized."
    Thus, the Emir answered his mother's words;
And she did not reject his good advice,
But like good earth which has received some seed,   230
And brings forth fruit at once, she spoke as follows:
"For you, son, I'll believe in the Trinity,
Go gladly with you to Romania,
Be baptized for remission of my faults,
Confessing thanks I've seen the light through you."   235
    Then likewise all his kinsmen who were there,
And all the rest who came with her, a crowd,
As with one voice cried out, confessing Christ:
    "We're coming with you to Romania,
And be baptized to attain eternal life!"   240
The Emir admired their readiness, and said:
"Glory to Thee, the only loving God,
Who willest not the death of any sinner,
But waitest his return to Thee with pity,
To make all men the partners of Thy kingdom!"   245
    Then, taking countless wealth along with them,
They set out for Romania together,
And when they came to parts of Cappadocia,

[29]

The Emir conferred with his Companions thus:
"A thought has come to me, my valiant soldiers, 250
Of going ahead myself to give my greeting,
For if another goes, I shall be called
Reluctant and indifferent by my love."
They answered it was good for him to do this,
For it was right that love be satisfied. 255
So, when he'd thought of what he'd planned to do,
He changed at once, and put on Roman dress:
A marvelous tabard that was gold besprinkled,
Purple and white silk, griffin ornamented,
A precious white turban with gold initials, 260
He rode upon a swift mule marked with a star,
And took with him three of his Companions.
Then, as they say, he flew, and reached the house,
Raising at once a cry filled full of joy:
"My most delightful dove, receive your hawk, 265
And give him comfort from his foreign travel!"
  Now at this cry the lady's maids peeked out,
And when they saw him, spoke thus to their mistress:
"Rejoice, rejoice, madame! Our master's come!"
But she thought this was unbelievable, 270
For he who suddenly gets what he wishes,
Thinks, from excess of joy, he sees a dream.
She said to the maids, "Do you think you see phantoms?"
And would have said a lot of things like that,
But suddenly she saw the young man coming, 275
Was overwhelmed with faintness from excitement,
And wrapping both her arms around his neck,
She hung there speechless, without shedding tears.
The Emir likewise became like one possessed,
And flinging the girl upon his breast, embraced her, 280
And thus they stayed entwined for many hours.
Had not the General's wife drenched them with water,
They would have fallen to the ground with faintness,
For love beyond all measure breeds such evils,
And overpowering love may lead to death, 285

[30]

A thing that they were just about to suffer.
But they could barely tear the two apart,
For the Emir kept kissing the girl's eyes,
Embracing her, and asking with delight:
"How are you, sweetest light, delightful lamb?   290
How are you, dearest soul, my consolation,
My charming dove, my graceful, blooming tree
With your own blossom, my belovéd child?"
And then the girl, her passionate love reviving,
Spoke sweetly in this fashion to the Emir: 295
"Welcome, my hope, the respite of my life,
My chief defender and my soul's delight.
All's well with us, thanks to the power of God,
Who thought us fit to see each other again.
But, tell me, master, how go things with you?"   300
"All's well," he answered, "by the grace of Christ,
Who lighted up my kin's and mother's hearts,
And led them to the light of knowing God.
You'll see them coming here in just a little."
And then he took his child up in his arms,   305
And spoke thus from the bottom of his heart:
"When, my fair hawk, will you unfold your wings,
And hunt the partridge, and subdue the robbers?"
Thus the Emir was speaking to his child.
But everyone had learned about his coming,   310
And ran to the house to say congratulations.
There is no way to tell how great their joy was.
They organized in groups, and started dancing;
And to this joy another joy was added,
For someone came to announce his mother's coming.   315
Then men and women all were to be seen
Going with the General's wife to meet her,
So one could hardly count them all with ease.
It was a work of true love, a strange wonder.
Who would not be amazed? Who would not marvel   320
To learn exactly how the powers of love
Brought aliens to unite in the one faith.

[31]

When they were near, at once they all dismounted,
And closely questioned them to learn about them.
The girl asked questions of her mother-in-law,   325
And then rejoicing kissed her relatives.
The horses pranced in joy with one another,
And joy for all was greater than before.
   They reached the house where they had held the wedding,
And the Emir himself baptized his mother,   330
And sponsored her in her regeneration,
And likewise all her kinsmen who came with her,
And was their father in the Holy Spirit.
Delight, that universal joy, grew greater,
The son rejoicing in his mother's faith,   335
The mother happy in her dearest son.
The Emir divided off part of his house,
And gave it to his relatives to live in.
The child, the Two-Blood Border Lord, was growing,
Having from God the wondrous grace of courage,   340
So all who looked upon him were astounded,
And marveled at his wit and noble daring.
His reputation spread throughout the world.

FOURTH BOOK

[*Of the Border Lord's Marriage*]

[*Encomium and recapitulation. Basil's education and first
hunt. He sees, woos and runs off with the General's daughter,
pursued by all the household. He kills all but the General
and his sons, and begs the General to accept him as son-in-
law. The wedding. Afterwards he lives on the border where
the Emperor comes to see him and honor him.*]

G-iv

The exploits of the Border Lord start here:
Both how he carried off that lovely maiden,
And all about his wedding, in this Fourth Book.

At once I shall remind you of Desire,
For it's the root and origin of Love   5
From which is born Affection and then Passion,
Which, growing bit by bit, brings forth such fruits
As constant cares, anxieties and worries,
Immediate pressing dangers, parting from parents.
For youth when in full bloom tears at our hearts,   10
Then recklessly attacks things unattempted:
To reach the sea, be undismayed by fire.
Dragons and lions and all other beasts
A steadfast passion reckons naught at all,
Considers even daring thieves as nothing,   15
Thinks nights are days, and mountain passes plains,
That wakefulness is rest, and far things near;
And many men deny their faith for passion.
Let none of you think this incredible;
I'll set a laudable witness in your midst,   20
The noble Emir, the prince of Syria,

[33]

So charming, handsome, with such savage daring,
Of most amazing size and well-bred strength,
And rather thought to be a second Samson.
For Samson rent a lion with his hands,   25
While the Emir slew countless hordes of lions.
    Record not Homer; nor Achilles' tales,
Nor Hector's; they are false. And Alexander
The Macedonian, mighty in purpose,
Was master of the world with God's assistance.   30
For with firm purpose he acknowledged God
From whom he had his valor and his daring.
But of old Philopappos, Ioannakes,
Or Kinnamos there's nothing worth the telling,
For they just boasted, but accomplished nothing.   35
But this man's deeds are true and well attested:
Ambron his grandsire, Karoës his uncle.
They gave three thousand chosen lancers to him;
He quelled all Syria and captured Kufah,
Then came to places in Romania,   40
Seized castles in the land of Heracles,
And plundered Charizané and Cappadocia.
He carried off the Ducas' charming daughter
Because of her great beauty and fine figure,
Denying everything, both faith and fame,   45
Becoming Orthodox, a Christian, for her;
The one-time foe appeared the slave of Romans.
To them a really lovely child was born
Who was named Basil from his very birth
And also Two-Blood from his parentage,   50
A pagan father and a Roman mother.
He became fearsome, as this tale will show,
And was named Border Lord from conquering borders.
Antakinos, one of the Kinnamades,
His grandsire, died, exiled by the Emperor,   55
Basil the Blesséd, mighty Border Lord.
His future had been bright, his fame immense;
All thought he was an excellent general.

[34]

His grandam was the General's wife, a Ducas;
His uncles were his mother's wondrous brothers
Who fought in single combat for their sister
Against the marvelous Emir, his father.
Thus he sprang from a race of noble Romans,
And was admired for his bravery.
   So let us now begin to tell his deeds.   65
This Basil, then, the wonderful Border Lord,
Was given by his father to a teacher
In childhood, spending three whole years in lessons,
And, with his sharp mind he acquired much learning.
Then, wanting horsemanship and also hunting,   70
He spent each day on these things with his father.
And so one day he said this to his father:
"The wish, master and father, is in my soul
To test myself in warring with the beasts.
So, if you really love Basil, your son,   75
Let us go out some place where there are beasts,
And you'll quite see the thought that's troubling me."
Hearing such words from his belovéd son,
The father was exalted, cheered to hear it,
And with much pleasure covered him with kisses.   80
"O best belovéd son, O soul and heart,
Your words are wonderful, your wish is sweet,
Although it's not yet time for fighting beasts.
For war on beasts is very terrible,
And you're a boy of twelve, one dozen years,   85
Entirely unfit for fighting beasts.
Do not, my sweetest son, have this in mind,
Nor pick your lovely rose before its time.
But when, God willing, you're a full grown man,
Why, then, without a word, you may fight beasts."   90
And when the noble lad had heard these words,
He grieved a great deal, and his heart was wounded,
And with tears in his eye, said to his father:
"If I do noble deeds after I'm grown,
What use is it to me? All men do that.   95

I want fame now to make my lineage shine.
I'll satisfy you too, my benefactor,
That you will have a big, brave servant in me
To be your succor and your aid in war."
His father assented to the young man's zeal,   100
For nobleness of nature shows from childhood.

   The next morning he took his brother-in-law,
The one born latest, golden Constantine.
And took his son, the noble Border Lord,
And certain horsemen too from his Companions,   105
And went straight from the marsh up to the woods
Where from afar they saw ferocious bears;
There were a male, a female and two cubs.
His uncle cried, "Now Basil, let me watch you!
Take nothing but your club; carry no sword,   110
For fighting bears with swords is not commended."
It was a strange and awesome sight to see,
For when he heard his uncle's voice, the boy
Dismounted right away, loosened his belt,
Took off his tunic, for the heart was great,   115
Fastened his skirts up firmly to his belt,
Put a camel's hair cap upon his head,
And then like lightning jumped out of his cuirass,
Carrying nothing but a simple staff.
He had great strength, and speed to go with it.   120
Now when they had approached close to the bears,
The female, jealous of her cubs, met him,
And loudly bellowing, came out towards him,
He inexperienced in fighting beasts,
Did not swing back so he could use his club,   125
But attacked quickly, caught her by the middle,
And squeezing with his arms, he strangled her
So that her entrails all came out of her mouth.
The male ran out again into the marsh.
His uncle called, "Don't let him get away, son!"   130
In his great hurry he had dropped his club,
So, flying like an eagle, he caught the beast.

The bear turned on him, opened its mouth wide,
And rushed to gobble down the youngster's head.
But the boy quickly seized it by the jowl,   135
Shook the beast, killed it, threw it on the ground,
Twisting its neck so that he broke its spine,
And straightway it expired in the young man's hands.
   Stirred by the bears' roars and their pounding feet,
A hind jumped up out of the covert's midst.   140
The Emir remarked, "Look, son, what is before you!"
He heard his father, went off like a panther,
And in a few strides caught up with the hind,
And grasping hold of it by the hind legs,
Shook it apart and tore it in two pieces.   145
Who would not marvel at God's mighty gifts,
Extolling his incomparable might?
Truly, it was a strange, astounding deed
For a boy without a horse to catch a hind,
And kill the bears with nothing in his hands;   150
Truly, a gift from God, from his right hand.
O lovely feet that are a match for wings,
That strangely beat the speed of a gazelle,
And overcame the might of fearsome beasts!
   Those who were there then, and who saw this marvel,   155
Said in astonishment to one another:
"Mother of God, this youth is quite a sight!
He is no human being from this earth;
God sent him forth for all the valorous
To see how he takes pleasure, fights and runs."   160
While his father and uncles talked together,
A mighty lion came up from the reed bed,
And then turned quickly around to watch the boy,
And saw him in the marsh, dragging the beasts.
With his right hand he dragged the bears he'd killed,   165
And with his left hand he was dragging the hind.
His uncle said to him, "Come hither, son,
And leave the dead behind; we've others living
On which even the nobles' sons are tested."

[37]

The boy replied to him, saying as follows: 170
"If God, who approves all things, so wills, and if
I have my father's and my mother's prayer,
You'll see him dead, just as you see the bears."
And with no sword he rushed to attack the lion.
Then his uncle said to him, "Take your sword.   175
This is no hind that you can tear apart."
And the young man at once spoke to him thus:
"Uncle and master, God is surely able
To put him in my hands just like the other."
Grasping his sword, he turned toward the beast.   180
And when he had come near, the lion sprang,
Lashing his tail, and beating his sides with it,
And roaring loudly at the youth, attacked.
The boy, however, raising his sword up high,
Struck him upon the head, full to the middle.   185
His head was split right to the shoulders below.
Then the Two-Blood spoke to his uncle thus:
"You see, my golden master, how great God is!
Lies he not silent, dead like the two bears?"
And then his father and his uncle kissed him   190
Upon his hands and arms, his eyes and chest,
And both rejoicing, spoke to him as follows:
"All who observe your handsome form and beauty,
O most desired boy, shall never doubt,
But truly will accept your daring feats."   195
   Indeed the young man was a handsome figure:
Blond hair a little curly, great big eyes,
A white and rosy face, and jet black eyebrows,
A breast like crystal, a full fathom wide.
His father looked at him exulting much,   200
And said to him with pleasure and delight:
"The heat is great, and it is midday now.
Even the beasts are hiding in the marsh.
So come, let us depart to the cool water,
And you shall wash the sweat off of your face,   205
And change your clothing too, for it is dirty

From the beasts' foaming and the lion's blood.
I am thrice-blest in having such a son,
So I shall wash your feet with my own hands.
Henceforth I can relieve my soul of care,   210
And so not worry about where I send you,
Whether on raids or enemy outposts."
   And so they all went to the spring at once.
Its water was astounding, cold as snow.
They sat in a circle while some washed his hands,   215
And some his face, and likewise some his feet.
The spring ran over; they drank thirstily,
That they might thus become as brave as he.
And then the young man changed his clothing too,
And donned some scanty garments to be cool.   220
The upper one was red with golden hems
The hems were decorated with fine pearls;
The neck was stuffed with lavender and musk.
It had enormous pearls instead of buttons;
The buttonholes were braided from pure gold.   225
He wore fine leggins, griffin ornamented;
His spurs were twined about with precious stones,
And on the gold work he had rubies too.
The noble youth was full of eagerness
To go to his mother lest she grieve for him,   230
And was compelling everyone to mount.
He saddled up a horse white as a dove,
Its forelock interlaced with precious stones
With little bells of gold amidst the stones,
So many little bells they made a noise   235
That was delightful and astounded all.
A green and red silk sheet upon its quarters
Covered the saddle, keeping dust away.
Its gear was braided with gold ornaments,
And all the saddlery was decked with pearls.   240
His horse was spirited and bold in play,
And yet the boy was clever riding it.
Whoever saw him marveled at the youth,

[39]

And how his horse played at the young man's will,
How like an apple on a tree he sat.   245
And then they hurried to go home again.
In front went the Companions all in order,
Behind him were his uncle and his father,
The youth between, all flashing like the sun,
And brandishing his lance in his right hand,   250
A green Arabian lance with golden pennon.
He was a lovely sight, pleasant to meet,
Musk to the senses, fragrant to the scent.
    Upon the way was the great General's house,
And when he had come near it, he called out: 255
"When a young man adores a lovely maiden,
And sees her beauty just as he is leaving,
His heart is tamed, he cares no more to live."
When those within the house heard his sweet song,
They were bemused as was Odysseus once   260
When on his ship he heard the Sirens' song.
Nor did the girl stay heedless of the youth,
That beautiful, renowned and famous maiden
Of dazzling beauty and distinguished family
With substance and with lands and other wealth   265
Impossible to reckon or imagine.
Her house alone was quite beyond all praise,
For it was gold and marble, all mosaic.
The separate chamber where the maiden lived
Was gold outside and covered with mosaic,   270
And also it was named the Maiden's Chamber.
    Accordingly, this wealthy, lovely maiden
Beheld the youth, and just as I was saying,
Her heart was burned, she cared no more to live.
A pain was kindled in her, as was normal,   275
For beauty is so sharp its arrow wounds,
And through the eyes themselves, reaches the soul.
She wished that she could tear her eyes away,
But couldn't bear to let his beauty go:
He drew her eyes, and they were plainly beaten.   280

And so she whispered to her lady's maid,
"Peek out, dear maid, and see the lovely youth;
Observe his beauty and unusual stature.
If my lord took him as his son-in-law,
Believe me, he'd have one like no one else!"   285
She stayed, and from the window watched the boy,
And the young man, not knowing this, inquired,
"Whose is this great and most impressive house?
Is this the General's whose fame they tell,
Whose daughter, widely praised, resides within?"   290
"Yes, my dear boy," his father answered him,
"And many noble Romans have perished for her."
"How did they perish, Father?" asked the boy.
"They wished to carry off the girl, my son,
Because of her great beauty, so they say.   295
The General, the maiden's father, knew this,
Set traps for them, and captured every one.
Some he beheaded, others still he blinded;
He has great power and glory in the land."
The Two-Blood sighed, and to his father said,   300
"Pray, Father, that I do not think to steal her,
For I have never been alarmed by traps.
No, this alone I pray, if you approve it:
Tell the General you are for our marriage
If he'd be pleased with me as a son-in-law,   305
And be my father-in-law of his own will.
If not, then let him know what will ensue!"
"I have informed him often, my dear son,
But he's not quite persuaded to consent."
Now while his father spoke thus to his son,   310
The young man spied the maiden through the window.
When he had looked at her, he stepped no closer,
But stood amazed, his heart all quivering.
He spurred his charger, and approached the girl,
And quietly he spoke to her as follows,   315
"Inform me, maid, if you have me in mind,
And if you'd like me to take you as my wife;

[41]

For if your mind's elsewhere, I will not press you."
And then the girl turned to her maid, and asked,
"Go down, good maid, and say to the young man,   320
'I tell you in God's name, you fill my heart,
But I don't know your family, young man.
If you are Basil, the Two-Blood Border Lord,
You come from very wealthy noble people,
And kinsmen of ours through the Ducases.   325
And yet my father has set watch on you,
For he has often heard of your exploits.
Beware, young man, lest you're imperiled through me,
And are deprived of your attractive youth,
For my unmerciful father will not spare you."   330
At once the youth responded to the girl,
"Lean out, my darling; let me see your beauty,
And let vast love for you enter my heart.
I'm young, you see; I don't know what desire is,
Nor understand about the ways of love.   335
But if desire for you comes to my soul,
The General, your father, and his kinsmen,
And all those with him, even were they arrows
And swords of flashing lightning, cannot harm me."
There was no end in sight to all their talk.   340
Then passion urged them to ignoble things,
For passion is master and enslaves the mind,
Subdues the sense as charioteers do horses;
And thus the lover has no self-restraint,
And no embarrassment before his neighbors,   345
But, as a slave of love, is wholly shameless.
Even the well-bred girl felt this way then,
And leaned part way out of the golden window.
The beauty of her face hindered his vision;
He couldn't see the sun-born maiden well,   350
For rays of light rose up out of her face
Which truly looked just like a painted picture,
With bright glad eye and yellow curly hair,
Her brows were black, their darkness unrelieved,

Her face like snow, and in the middle tinted   355
As if with the fine purple emperors honor.
Seeing her thus, that marvelous young man,
Was smitten to the soul, and hurt in heart.
He felt unending pain, and stood distressed.
Now when the noble maiden saw him thus,   360
She didn't let him stay in misery long,
But very quickly sent her love to him,
Filling him with much joy mingled with pleasure;
And giving him her ring, she said to him:
"Depart rejoicing, lad, and don't forget me!"   365
Hiding it in the bosom of his robe,
He answered quickly, "Wait for me tomorrow!"
Then, filled with joy, he left with all his men.
When he reached home, he straightway became worried,
And he entreated God with all his heart: 370
"O God and Master, listen to my prayer.
Make the sun set for me, and make the moon rise,
That it may be my helper in this task,
Because I wish to go ahead alone."
And privately he spoke to his stud groom: 375
"Unsaddle my charger; saddle up the black
With double girths and double martingales;
And hang my fine sword-club upon my saddle;
And use a heavy bit for turning quickly."
   When called to dinner, he could eat no food,   380
Nor would he have a taste of drink at all.
The girl was on his mind; he saw her beauty.
At times hopeless, he had no wish for her,
But thought at other times his chances good.
He seemed to all like one who watched a dream.   385
His mother even halted him, and wondered,
"What's happened to you, child? You grieve my soul.
Has some beast bothered you? some fear disturbed?
Some fiend, seeing your bravery, bewitched you?
Tell me at once, and don't distress my soul,   390
For he who hides disease is ruined by it."

[43]

"No beast has bothered me," the young man answered,
"No turmoil either has disturbed my soul.
If someone has bewitched me, I won't curse her
Who did no wrong, but I myself am well." 395
Then standing up, he mounted to his chamber,
Taking his boots with him, and got his lute.
At first he touched the strings with his bare hands
(He was well taught on instruments of music),
And having tuned it, struck it, softly singing: 400
"Who loves a lass nearby does not lose sleep,
But he whose love's far off must not waste nights.
My love is far away, so let us hasten,
And not grieve her who lies awake for me."
Now when the sun had set, and the moon took over, 405
He rode alone, but carrying his lute.
His horse was fiery, and the moon like day.
At dawn he came up to the maiden's chamber.
   She'd waited for him, wakeful all the night,
But at the dawn relaxed and fell asleep. 410
So when the noble young man failed to see her,
He was sorely distressed and greatly troubled,
And grievous thoughts were hammering his heart;
He had intolerable woe and pain.
And to himself he said, "Has she repented? 415
Is she afraid perchance her parents notice?
What shall I plan for that? How learn the truth?
My mind's in doubt. There's nothing I can do.
For if I speak, and others hear me calling,
Then those on guard here will suspect and strike. 420
Caught in the act, I should not meet my dearest;
Just seeing my belovéd would be hard.
What use is there to live a life like that?"
So saying to himself, and much bewildered,
He thought it would be best to strike his lute, 425
And make a trial of the things he feared.
"For safety's sake," he said, "I'll test the girl,
Putting this lute between us as my helper,

And then the will of God must come to pass."
He turned it, and he struck it with his plectrum,   430
Produced a pleasing tune, and softly sang
"How could you disregard, dear, our young love,
And fall sweetly asleep so unconcerned?
Arise, my lovely rose, my scented apple,
The morning star has risen. Come, let's go."   435
　　Now when the maiden heard the lute's sweet sound,
She jumped out of her bed, tightened her girdle,
And leaning far outside, said to the boy:
　　"I punished you, dear heart, for being late,
As I shall always do when you are careless.   440
And playing the lute! Don't you know where you are?
My dear, if Father knew, and injured you,
And you should die for me, oh what a crime!
For God, Who knows all secrets, understands
That love for you is rooted in my heart;   445
Your failure I consider my disaster,
So save yourself, my soul, before the light comes,
And always think of her who loves you best.
Because, my dear, I will not come with you.
I know desire, that strange delight, inflames you;   450
Reason is urging you to die for me.
But if you led me astray, and I came with you,
And if my brothers and my kin should know it,
And if my father and my people caught you,
How could you get me out, and save your life?"   455
Much grieved, the wondrous boy answered the girl:
"That you're upset, my lady, I commend,
And that you recognize just what will happen.
You judge the future well, reasoning clearly.
But still you do not know a thing about me,   460
For if you knew the deeds that I have done,
You would not say your brothers and your kinsmen
Would catch and hurl me down, and that you'd grieve.
So be this known to you, my soul, as certain,
That I alone expect to beat their troops,   465

[45]

Defeat their ranks, and overcome their power.
As for your father and all his Companions,
Likewise your brothers and your kinsmen too,
I reckon them mere infants, nothing at all.
I seek to learn just one thing from your lips: 470
Whether you are eager to go with me,
So we may leave the byways before daylight.
Brave men are killed in lanes and narrow places,
And cowards are made bold in open fields.
But if you've changed your mind, and choose another,   475
And therefore make excuses of that sort,
Then, by Saints Theodore, Christ's witnesses,
No other, while I live, shall be your husband!"
At once the radiant girl said to the youth:
"You, dearest, inexperienced at first,   480
But made of love and affection, as you said,
Suffer right now for me. Perhaps that's true;
For even I myself can likewise guess it.
And, though I shouldn't talk about myself,
Still, as desire enslaves me, I'll tell all.   485
Many great men and many well-born nobles,
Both kinsmen and the sons of kings, have sought me,
Men who have royal rank as well as raiment,
And who longed greatly to observe my features,
Have frequently approached close to my home,   490
But none at all would satisfy my father;
None were thought good enough to see my shadow,
None heard my voice at all, my conversation,
My laughter when I smiled, nor sound of footsteps.
I never put my head out of the window,   495
But kept myself invisible to strangers,
Except to kinsmen and my own close friends.
None ever saw the features of my face;
I kept the strictness that becomes us maidens.
Now I'm outside; I've gone beyond the limits,   500
And have become shameless for love of you.
And I, whom no strange man has ever seen,

[46]

Am now exchanging words quite shamelessly,
And the free spirit of virginity
Is now a slave, I see, suddenly shameless.   505
For from the hour I saw your face, young man,
It burned my prudent soul, as would the fire.
It changed my reason and likewise my judgment,
Made me immodest, and enslaved my spirit
To you alone, and to your love belovéd   510
Now I obey, and wish to go with you,
Deny my kin, become bereft of parents,
Estranged from brothers and from boundless wealth,
And go with you wherever you may bid,
Having God, Helper of us all, as witness   515
And best avenger should you lead me astray.
Love burns you, and desire is spurring you,
Reason persuades you you should die for me,
A thing I pray I'll never see or hear of."
    While she spoke thus, the lovely maiden's eyes   520
Brimmed over with her tears; she deeply sighed,
And blamed herself for being very shameless.
But, though she greatly wished to change her mind,
The boundless passion in her would not let her.
There's power in passion, in desire and love.   525
These keep their proper order most precisely.
A man is temperate; desire attacks him;
And then this lover has no self-restraint,
No shame before his kin, no fear of neighbors,
But is all shameless and the slave of love.   530
Thus too these fair young folks were suffering.
The marvelous youth observed the maid was weeping,
And said to her in turn, himself in tears:
"Fair maiden, I myself know all about you,
The boundless wealth your father has acquired,   535
For which so many nobles longed to take you.
So I have sought to know the facts precisely,
For I, my dearest, am not seeking wealth.
I wish no property, and want no glory,

[47]

Count all as dross, delighting in your beauty.   540
For from the hour, dark-eyes, we saw each other,
You were not absent from my soul one second,
Rooted within, and intertwined with it.
I dream and see you when you are not here.
I've never fallen in love with any beauty,   545
Nor have I known the ways of love at all.
Come, my sweet light, accompany your lover,
Reveal the love you have concealed within you,
For the clear proof of it consists in deeds,
And with God's will we'll live in joy together.   550
Your parents too will be delighted by this
When they know what a son-in-law they've met with,
And none will blame you, but will call you blesséd."
This and much else besides the young man said.
"In you is my beginning and my end;   555
Begun with God, until my death," he said,
"And should I ever wish, my soul, to grieve you,
And not preserve your love for me untarnished—
A most pure passion—up until my death,
May I not die a Christian, not succeed,   560
May I not earn the prayers of my own parents.
And you, most noble maid, keep like resolve!"
    With these words ringing in her ears, the maid said:
"Even if surrendering myself was wrong
(Indeed, good order is called nobility,   565
Which I have breached, I don't know why I did it),
Yet my pure passion and sure love for you
Persuaded me your love was preferable."
Thus, with a vow of love, the maiden spoke:
"I've left my home, my parents and my brothers   570
And with God's help, I trust myself to you, lad.
Take Him for witness that you will not grieve me,
But make me a lawful wife until the end.
For truly many lovers break their word,
Though first they seem to love those they desire."   575
Surprised when he heard this, the boy admired

[48]

The virgin's sense; but just the same he vowed,
"By Father, Son, and by the Holy Spirit,
I will not grieve you ever, noble maid,
But make you my own lady and my mistress,   580
Both wife and house companion till life's end,
If you will keep your passion for me pure,
Just as I said before, my dearest soul."
    When they'd confirmed each other in their vows,
The maiden leaned out of her golden window,   585
And rising on his horse, the young man took her;
The partridge flew away; the falcon caught her.
They kissed each other with delight, of course,
Unutterably happy and both weeping,
For they had found a moment of great joy,   590
And ardently were shedding tears of pleasure.
Indeed, the boy, stirred up by joy and courage,
Stood opposite the house, and loudly cried:
"Pray, father-in-law, for me and for your daughter,
And thank God you have such a son-in-law."   595
    Now when the General's sentries heard this cry,
They loudly gave the call for all to mount.
Suddenly hearing this, the General,
Beside himself, not knowing what to do,
Cried out in anguish, "I have lost my light!   600
My only daughter's gone out of my sight!"
And when the General's wife heard this, she cried,
"My only daughter's carried off, and gone!"
Her brothers, who were elsewhere, mourned and cried,
"Who can have dared to do this lawless thing?   605
Who took our sister suddenly from us?"
The housemaids wept and cried aloud and wailed.
The place was filled with unrestrained laments.
A mighty force in arms pursued the youth;
The General rode behind with his two sons.   610
Nor was the General's wife left in the house.
She couldn't bear to part from her own daughter;
In fact she took a crowd of housemaids with her,

[49]

And followed weeping, hair unbound, on foot.
"Dear soul," she cried, "I don't know where you're going!"   615
And no one, either old or young, remained
Who did not ride in pursuit of the young man,
All sorely grieving at the maid's abduction.
There were so many none could count exactly.
   Just as the light of day was growing bright,   620
They overtook them down in the dark plains.
The lovely maiden saw them from afar,
For she was looking back, and watching keenly
While held close in the arms of her belovéd,
And spoke these words to him, clutching him tightly: 625
"Exert yourself, dear, lest they separate us;
And whip the black horse on with all your strength.
Look, our pursuers are about to catch us!"
When he heard this, that marvelous young man
Was filled with courage, and turning from the road,   630
He found a double tree which had two branches,
And set the girl down in between the branches.
"Sit there, my lovely one, and watch your darling,"
And then straightway he armed himself completely.
Then said the sun-born maiden to the boy,   635
"Take care you do no injury to my brothers!"
   Then a strange thing was shown to those there present:
All by himself he dared encounter thousands,
And in a short time slaughtered countless soldiers,
All fully armed and mounted, trained for war.   640
He first advised them to turn back again,
And not to undertake to test his valor,
But they, ashamed to have one man defeat them,
Preferred to die instead of being shamed.
He started forward, drawing out his sword-club,   645
And, ere the General came, not one was left.
Then, finally finished with his war, the boy
Came back, a victor, to the girl, rejoicing,
Got off his horse, and kissed her countless times:
"Delightful girl, you've proof of deeds in me."   650

[50]

The maid herself admiring him still more,
Accepted with delight his noisy kisses,
And spoke to the boy quietly as follows:
"Don't injure my own brothers, dearest soul;
For those whom you see coming towards us now   655
I judge to be my brothers, from their horses;
The third man who is with them is my father.
Return them to me safe; keep them unharmed."
"It shall be as you wish," he told the girl,
"Unless some unexpected thing occurs,   660
For he who spares his foes in time of war
Is often slain unfeelingly by them."
Saying these words he leaped upon his horse,
And fell on those around the General.
The brothers of the maiden, filled with zeal,   665
Told their companions that they should destroy him,
Planning that other hands should murder him.
The boy observed his dearest one's behest,
Attacked with skill, and wisely killed them all.
The brothers charged down on him furiously.   670
He circled them, and threw them from their horses
So neatly that he did not harm nor wound them.
Then turning toward the General, he dismounted,
Clasped his hands tight, and bowing low to him,
Began to speak to him with a bold look: 675
"Forgive me, master. Do not censure me.
Your troops are clods the way they strike and parry,
And therefore most of them have gone to Hell.
But I'm not of ignoble, coward stock,
And so if you will bid me do you service,   680
You'll be assured about your son-in-law.
And if you'll test me strictly by my deeds,
You'll often bless yourself for your good fortune."
At once the General raised his hands on high,
And looking towards the east, gave thanks to God: 685
"Glory to Thee, God; all that profits us
Thou orderest with inexpressible wisdom.

[51]

For I'm vouchsafed the son-in-law I wished,
Handsome and well born, temperate and brave,
Such as none ever found in the whole world."
With all his heart he thus gave thanks to God,
And, as was meet, he spoke thus to the boy:
"My son-in-law, above all else thank God
Who ordereth what profits well for us.
Accept, fair youth, her whom you longed to have.
Unless you'd had such boundless passion for her,
You'd not have dared to march alone on thousands.
So come, let us go back into my house;
And do not think you'll suffer hurt from us,
For it's to make arrangements for the wedding,
Contracts in writing in your father's presence.
You'll quickly be advised to come back to us,
And take away with you my daughter's dowry.
I'll make your marriage known throughout the world,
So you may have your dowry on that day.
It's twenty hundredweight of ancient coins,
A clothes chest valued at five hundred pounds,
Which long ago I specially set aside
In my belovéd's name; and silver vessels,
Much real estate with rents, thirty-six pieces;
Seventy handmaids and her mother's house
Which was most notable and truly precious;
Likewise her mother's superb jewelry,
Her world-famed crown, an admirable work
Assembled out of gold and precious stones;
And with all these the animals found there,
Four hundred champions and eighty grooms,
And fourteen cooks, and just as many bakers,
One hundred fifty other slaves as well.
I'll honor you above my other children,
Give boundless wealth and not a few estates,
Provide with these more things than those I've mentioned
Before the sacred rite occurs, my son.
I'll make your marriage known throughout the world.

690
695
700
705
710
715
720

Youths shall not say you sought illicit union,   725
And carried off a girl who had no fortune,
A shameful thing to all right-minded men.
These charges you can't easily escape
Unless you come back home with us right now.
Thus too my wife may have some consolation—   730
She doesn't know what sort you are at all—
And glorify the Giver of good things.
So heed, good son-in-law, and come with me."
So spoke the General, and flattered him.
The youth at once answered the General: 735
"To heed your counsel, which is excellent,
Is right for me, master and father-in-law.
I fear though there is danger in it for me,
That from your shame I'll owe a pitiful death
As foe, a treacherous former foe, of yours.   740
Conscience persuades me to the opposite,
And I should blush to see your lady's face.
My lord and father-in-law, it was my wish
To take your daughter for her beauty's sake,
And not because of wealth or her estates.   745
All these things I present to my wife's brothers.
Her beauty satisfies me more than dowries,
For God provides both wealth and poverty,
Both humbles and exalts, brings down and raises.
As for returning, I'll not disobey you,   750
But let me go back to my mother first,
So that my father may see the bride-to-be,
And glorify the Lord. I'll come back quickly.
But don't regret this; give your blessing rather,
For we're your children, servants of your soul."   755
The General admired the youth's good sense.
"May God," he said, "give you His blessing, son,
And grant you to enjoy your years of life."
He embraced the youth, and mounted on his horse.
The youth went to the girl, the General home;   760
His sons, because of their fall, went back with him,   .

[53]

Marveling greatly at the young man's valor.
　But now this truly marvelous young man
Came to the place in which the maiden waited.
"Come hither, sweetest light," he called, and said,   765
"Come hither, sweetest flower, fragrant rose;
Come hither, heifer of mine, whom love has yoked.
Let us be on our way, for no one hinders.
There's no one, lovely maid, who bars our passage.
Your father and brothers are the sole survivors   770
Because I had regard for your injunction."
The girl descended from the tree at once,
Overflowing with pleasure and with joy,
And quietly she walked to meet the boy.
Then, coming close to him, she asked with feeling: 775
"No accidents at all befell you, darling,
So tell me quickly all about my brothers."
"Don't worry, dearest soul," the boy replied,
"None but your father's praiseworthy Companions
Has suffered hurt at all, not even slightly."   780
He stooped and lifted her up on his horse,
Taking her right up with him on his own horse.
Delightedly they took their fill of kisses,
Going upon their way with joy and pleasure.
And when his father's sentries noticed him   785
Bearing the rosy maiden in his arms,
They ran with haste to give congratulations.
And when his father heard of his arrival,
He mounted horse at once, filled with great joy.
His wife's five brothers and three thousand men   790
Prepared twelve women's saddles and twelve bridles,
And two of them with pearls were ornamented,
The rest with animals engraved on gold.
The saddles all were beautifully draped;
The horses all were covered with silk sheets   795
Beneath which they were hidden with much gold.
Both bugles and bass trumpets were behind them,
Drums and instruments played fortissimo;

The noise at that time could be heard for miles.
When they had come within three miles of the house,   800
The lovely maiden saw them from afar,
And trembled, for she did not recognize them,
And said to the young men worriedly,
"If they are strangers, they will separate us."
"Don't be afraid, sweet light," the boy replied,   805
"It is your father-in-law, who's pleased to come here."
In turn the sun-born maid said to the youth,
"I am ashamed, my soul, for I'm alone.
If you'd obeyed my father, and returned,
I'd have my maids and all my things here now;   810
Your father ought to know whose girl you've taken.
But you made the decision: you explain!"
"Don't grieve, my lady, that you are alone,
For they all know you, even if you are.
You can't be blamed at all because of that."   815
When they drew near, they greeted one another.
The youth got off his horse with his belovéd;
The Emir dismounted, and embraced them both.
"My son," he said, "may God, to bless you both,
Grant many years of life in peace and plenty,   820
Admitting you as sharers in His kingdom."
They set the girl upon the gold wrought saddle,
And placed a precious wreath upon her head,
And each of her relations who was there
Pressed many truly precious gifts upon her.   825
They adorned the boy too as a young man should be,
Then sounded trumpets, and returned again.
They sounded bugle calls, and beat their drums,
Played instruments, and singing many songs,
They made all sorts of music with their lutes,   830
And quickly they returned home celebrating.
The joy they felt was so superlative
Who can interpret it, or who can tell?
It even seemed as if the very ground
They walked upon rejoiced while they were walking.   835

And everyone who chanced upon their gladness
Became beside himself with the rejoicing.
The hills were leaping and the rocks were dancing,
The rivers gushing and the trees exulting,
The very air was brightened by rejoicing.   840
    When they were just about to reach the house,
An endless crowd of women came to meet them.
The General's wife came out to meet the young ones,
The Border Lord's delightful mother with her.
And comely housemaids brilliantly adorned,   845
Some bearing flowers, roses, myrtle wreaths,
The fragrance of their smell scenting the air;
And others clashing cymbals while they sang
A very pleasant song that praised the boy,
The virgin with him, and their parents too.   850
The ground was strewn with myrtle and sweet bay,
Narcissus, roses, many fragrant flowers.
The mother-in-law fondly embraced the bride,
Presenting generously her finest work;
Her pleasure and delight were quite unfeigned.   855
    When they came to the house, the Emir at once
Sent his wife's brothers and a host of troops,
Counting three thousand of his own Companions,
To tell the General to attend the wedding:
"I bid you, fellow father-in-law, to attend   860
This wedding God arranged, though we would not."
When he heard this, he left no stone unturned
To honor his belovéd ones, but took
A huge amount of gifts along with him,
And set out on the next day with his wife.   865
They had no word to say, no room to doubt,
Because they knew what sort of groom they'd found.
Therefore with eagerness and with great gladness
They went their way, and sang about the wedding,
And so did the girl's brothers and those with them.   870
When the boy's father heard of their arrival,
He went out with his people to give welcome.

The marvelous Emir wished to dismount;
The General implored, and tried to stop him.
When they'd embraced each other properly,   875
They hastened to the house; farther along
A countless host on foot came out to meet them,
And others came with these, a group of housemaids.
And now they reached the confines of the house,
Suitably decked with many fragrant stuffs,   880
Rosewater, and all other sorts of perfumes.
The lovely mother of the boy was leading.
What mind has quite the strength to tell what followed—
The wonderful reception by the Emir,
The lovely party given by his spouse,   885
The well-planned banquet and the right arrangements,
The endless spectacle of varied foods,
Servings of meat from countless animals,
The actors' changes, and the flutists' tunes,
The twirling dancing girls, their shifting feet,   890
The pleasure of the dances and strange music?
First one thing charmed, and then, in turn, another.
Next day the dowry contracts were completed.
The contents can't be set forth word for word,
But what they both agreed on for their children,   895
Estates that could be counted easily,
Are not unsuitable to list by name—
The number of their cattle and such things.
The General presented twelve black horses,
Twelve pleasant chargers that were beautiful,   900
Twelve choice mules with their saddles and their bridles
Of silver and cast gold, praiseworthy works;
And twelve young housemen, grooms with golden belts,
Twelve hunting leopards that were tried and proven,
A dozen snowy hawks from far Abasgia,   905
A dozen falconers and falcons also,
Two golden icons of Saints Theodore,
A gold-embroidered tent, immense and lovely,
With many stenciled shapes of animals;

[57]

The ropes were silken and the stakes were silver;   910
And two Arabian spears made out of dogwood,
As well as great Chosroës' famous sword.
These were the gifts the General presented
His son-in-law, the Two-Blood; and the Emir
Gave the girl a precious bridal gift.   915
The General's wife, the Border Lord's grandmother,
Likewise his wife's five brothers and his kin,
Gave him a pearl of infinite size, gold, gems,
And endless valuable purple silks.
The Two-Blood's mother-in-law likewise presented   920
A green and white silk scarf and precious girdles,
And four white turbans with gold monograms,
A golden robe with griffins on the back.
His wife's first brother gave him ten young men,
Castrated, handsome, and with lovely hair,   925
All clad in Persian garments made of silk
With fine gold sleeves that came up to their necks.
Her other brother gave a shield and lance,
His other relatives gave many things,
Although the kinds of things cannot be counted.   930
It took three months before the wedding ended;
But popular rejoicing did not end.
After the three months' wedding was accomplished,
The General took his relatives by marriage,
Even the groom himself, went to his house,   935
And had a wedding gayer than the first.
The General exulted as he noticed
The boy's well-ordered state, his prudent valor,
His gentle ways, and other good behavior.
The General's wife was glad to see his beauty   940
And stature, which was comely and exotic.
His wife's own brothers visited him often,
And always boasted of their own exploits—
Praise to the one good which fulfills the deed,
For in the governance of great affairs   945
God enters with us, let none disbelieve it.

[58]

So let us sensibly send thanks to God
Because He is the giver of all good things.
    So, after staying there for several days,
The Emir returned again to his own home,   950
And with him went the Two-Blood and his darling,
And once again there was a grand arrival.
Then, since the youth had shown that he was worthy,
And had become renowned for his exploits,
For he'd made good in almost all the world,   955
He chose to live alone upon the border,
And took his girl and his own servants with him.
He had an endless longing to live alone,
And walk around alone with no one with him.
In fact, where he had gone he had his own tent   960
In which he and the girl lived all alone.
Her two maidservants had another tent,
The Border Lord's Companions still another,
And each was a great distance from the others.
    Now many of the outlaws heard about this,   965
And hatched a plot to carry off the girl.
He overcame them, and he slew them all
Just as he conquered all of Babylon,
Tarsus, Baghdad, the Mavrochionites,
And other parts of the dread Ethiops' land.   970
    On hearing of these deeds, the Emperor
Who at that time was governing the Romans,
Basil the Blesséd, the great trophy winner,
Whose imperial fame was buried with him,
Chanced to be on campaign against the Persians   975
In those same places where the boy was living,
And when he heard about it was amazed.
So wishing greatly he might see the youth,
He sent a letter to him with these words:
"We've learned the stories of your many exploits,   980
My son, and we have much rejoiced in them,
And offered thanks to God who works with you.
Our purpose is to see you with our own eyes,

[59]

And give requital worthy of your deeds.
Come to us gladly, without hesitation,   985
And don't suspect you'll suffer hurt from us."
When he received this, he returned an answer:
"I am your majesty's most abject slave;
Indeed, I have no right to your good things.
Master, what deed of mine do you admire,   990
Who am so humble, base, and quite undaring?
Still, he who trusts in God can do all things.
Therefore, since you desire to see your servant,
Be by the Euphrates after a little while.
You'll see me all you wish, my sacred master.   995
Don't think that I refuse to come before you,
But you have certain inexperienced soldiers,
And if perhaps they say something they shouldn't,
I certainly would deprive you of such men,
For such things, master, happen to the young."   1000
    The Emperor read his letter word by word,
Admired the humbleness of the boy's statement,
And understood with pleasure his high courage.
    Since he wished strongly to behold the youth,
He took along with him a hundred soldiers,   1005
Some spearmen too, and went to the Euphrates,
Ordering all on no account to utter
A word offensive to the Border Lord.
Those posted to keep watch on his account
Shortly announced the Emperor's arrival   1010
To the marvelous Two-Blood Border Lord.
The Two-Blood came out all alone to meet him,
And bowed his head down to the ground, and said,
"Hail, you who take imperial power from God,
And rule us all because of the heathen's sins.   1015
Why has it happened that the whole world's master
Comes before me, who am of no account?"
The Emperor, astonished when he saw him,
Forgot the burden of his majesty,
Advanced a little from his throne, embraced him,   1020

Joyfully kissed him, and admired his stature,
And the great promise of his well-formed beauty.
"My son," he said, "you've proof of all your deeds;
The way you're put together shows your courage.
Would that Romania had four such men!   1025
So speak, my son, freely and openly,
And then take anything you wish from us."
"Keep everything, my lord," the boy replied,
"Because your love alone is enough for me.
It's not more blessèd to receive than give;   1030
You have immense expenses in your army.
So I beseech your glorious majesty:
Love him who is obedient, pity the poor,
Deliver the oppressed from malefactors,
Forgive those who unwittingly make blunders,   1035
And heed no slanders, nor accept injustice,
Sweep heretics out, confirm the orthodox.
These, master, are the arms of righteousness
With which you can prevail over all foes.
To rule and reign are not part of that power   1040
Which God and His right hand alone can give.
Vile as I am, I grant your majesty
To take what you once gave Iconium
As tribute, and as much again, from them.
Master, I'll make you carefree about this   1045
Until my soul shakes off this mortal coil."
    The Emperor was delighted at these words.
"O marvelous and excellent young man,"
He said, "we name you a patrician now,
And grant you all your grandfather's estates;   1050
We give to you the power to rule the borders,
And will confirm this with a golden bull,
And furnish you with rich imperial raiment."
    So spoke the Emperor. The youth at once
Ordered one of his wild, unbroken horses   1055
Brought before them, hobbled in iron chains.
He told his boys to release it: "Let it run!"

Fastened his skirts up firmly to his belt,
Then started running after it to catch it,
And in a little space he grasped its mane,   1060
And turned the big, wild beast around backwards,
Kicking and plunging, trying to escape.
When the boy came before the Emperor,
He threw it down, spread flat upon the ground.
All were astonished at the marvelous sight.   1065
He wished to leave. A lion from the grove
Came out, and startled those there present with him
(For there were many lions in that place),
And even the Emperor had turned to flee.
The boy ran up at once toward the lion,   1070
And seizing it by one of its hind legs,
He shook it hard, and dashed it to the ground,
Displaying it quite dead while all were watching.
Then in his hand, held like a hare, he brought it
Before the Emperor, and said, "Accept   1075
The game your servant hunted for you, master."
All were astonished and began to tremble;
They recognized his strength was superhuman.
The Emperor, with his hands stretched toward heaven,
Said, "Glory to Thee, Master, Maker of all things,   1080
Who made me worthy to see such a man,
Strong above all the present generation!"
He ordered the lion's skin to be picked up,
And made the boy a lot of promises.
They embraced each other, and at once withdrew,   1085
One to his troops, the other to his girl.
Thenceforth the story was confirmed by all:
The boy was called Basil the Border Lord
From the gold bull that he should rule the borders.

But at this point we're going to end the book,   1090
And keep what follows for another session.
A glut of talk, my theologian says,
Is always very hostile to good hearing.

[62]

FIFTH BOOK

[*About the Deserted Bride*]

[*The temptations of youth. Basil tells his story: He finds a
girl deserted at a spring in the desert, learns her story, beats
off robbers, takes her to find her seducer, but helps himself to
his reward on the way.*]

Youth surely is the age of vanity,
Reaching at that time toward unruly pleasures,
But he who guides it by the reins steadfastly,
Remains unconquered by his passions always.
He is made heir to the eternal life   5
Instead of to base, impious, transient pleasure.
The wanton can't achieve eternal life,
For just as fire can't be quenched with oil,
So neither can the wanton flee from sin
By which the fires are fed for the licentious.   10
    So too this wondrous noble Border Lord,
Who'd been enriched by all God's gracious gifts,
Having relaxed his own youth just a little,
Fell carelessly into adultery.
Then afterwards repenting of his act,   15
He told his sin to those he chanced to meet,
Not for the sake of boasting, but repentance.
    Therefore one day, meeting a Cappadocian,
And wishing to decry his own mistake,
He told his story, telling it quite fairly: 20
"When, as I wished, I parted from my father,
And chose to live alone upon the borders,
I wished to travel inside Syria,

[63]

My age at that time being fifteen years.
Now when I reached Arabia's arid plains,   25
Making my way alone, as was my wont,
Sitting my horse, and carrying my spear,
I became thirsty, for the heat was great,
And looked around for water everywhere.
I saw a tree off towards a swampy thicket,   30
And urged my horse on, thinking to find water,
And was not wrong: the tree there was a date palm,
And from its roots there rose a wondrous spring.
As I approached, I heard loud cries of grief
And wails of lamentation and much weeping.   35
The weeper was a very lovely girl.
Then I, thinking that I beheld a ghost,
Was frightened, and my hair stood up on end.
I drew the weapon out that always guards me,
Because the place was lonely, dense, and pathless.   40
Now when she saw me, she sprang up at once,
Wrapping herself in clothes in proper order,
Then wiped away the showers from her eyes,
And gladly started telling me as follows:
'Whence do you go alone, and whither sir?   45
Surely you too have not strayed here from love?
But since it seems you have been sent from God
To take poor wretched me out of the desert,
Rest yourself here a little while, my lord,
And hear my tale as well as I can tell it,   50
And give me consolation for my woes,
For grief is lifted from the soul by talking.'
   "When I heard this, my feelings turned to joy;
I knew the sight I'd seen was something real.
So I dismounted right away with pleasure,   55
Her inexpressible beauty touched my heart;
I thought her second only to my wife,
And so I tied my charger to a tree,
Then stood my lance up in between its roots,
And when I'd had some water, said to her: 60

[64]

'Tell me first, girl, why you are staying here,
And for what reason living in this desert?
Then you yourself shall learn who I am too.'
    "We sat together on a humble stool,
And she began to speak, and deeply sighed: 65
'My native place is Meferkéh, young man;
You've heard of Haplorrabdes, its emir.
He is my sire, Melanthia my mother.
I loved a Roman to my own undoing,
One whom my father held three years in chains.   70
He said he was a famous general's son.
I loosed his bonds and rescued him from prison,
I gave him horses, champions of my father's,
Made him a chief of Syria, my mother
Consenting, as my father was away,   75
For he was always busy with his wars.
Then he appeared to have much love for me,
And, if he didn't see me, nearly died.
But he was false, as the event made clear.
Indeed, one day when we'd considered flight,   80
He wished to go forth to Romania.
And told this wish to me, and how he feared
My father, if he ever should return.
He pressed me strongly to go forth with him,
And swore to me with awe-inspiring oaths,   85
He'd marry me, and he would not forsake me.
I trusted him, and said I'd fly with him.
Then both watched for an opportunity
To steal away the riches of my parents.
And then, by bitter devilish mischance,   90
Disease came to my mother, death was near her,
And all the others in the house ran out
Lamenting, as death drove them thus to tears.
But I, poor fool, found opportunity
To take much wealth, and left with the deceiver,   95
Night ministering coolly to the deed,
For it was moonless, and there was no light.

We mounted and began the way in haste
On horses that were ready in advance,
Fearful until we reached the three mile mark,   100
But when we'd passed it, recognized by none,
We finished all the rest, fearless but toiling.
And when the time required, we had some food,
And took our fill of sleep, and shared our food.
I blush to tell the secrets of our love,   105
And the affection which he showed to me.
He said I was his soul, light of his eyes,
And said I soon would be his wife, his darling,
Insatiately kissing while he held me.
   " 'Rejoicing in each other all the way   110
We came upon this fountain which you see,
And for three days and nights we rested here,
Insatiately making love's exchanges.
Then, though he kept his purpose hid within him,
The vile transgressor in him now appeared.   115
   " 'For while we slept together the third night,
He rose from bed in secret, saddled horses,
And carried off the gold and best equipment.
Now when I noticed when I rose from sleep,
I made me ready for the road at once,   120
Disguising my appearance in boys' garments,
For in this fashion I had left my country.
But now, what's more, he'd mounted on his own horse,
And leading mine, had started on the way.
So when I saw this desperate deception,   125
I ran, although on foot, after him, screaming,
"Where are you going, leaving me alone, dear?
Have you forgotten all I did for you?
Remember what we vowed right from the first?"
Then, when he didn't turn around, I cried,   130
"Have mercy! Pity me! Oh, save poor me!
Don't leave me here to be devoured by beasts!"
And much besides I said to him while weeping,
But he was gone from sight without a word.

My feet by now had given out completely,
Covered with blood from bruising on the stones,
And I fell down and sprawled just like a corpse.
By daytime I had only just recovered,
And came back to the spring, compelled to walk.
Now I'm bereft of all. I have no hope.   140
For I don't want to go back to my parents;
I'm shamed before my neighbors and companions.
I don't know where to find him who betrayed me,
And pray you'll put a knife into my hands;
I'll kill myself for acting senselessly.   145
For life is not worth living when all's lost.
Oh, what misfortunes and calamities!
I've been estranged from kin, parted from parents,
To gain a lover, and have failed to get him!'
    "Now while the girl was speaking thus and weeping,   150
Tearing her curly locks, beating her face,
I checked as best I could her lamentations,
And drew her hands back from her hair a bit,
Exhorting her to have more worthy hopes.
And to find out, I asked, 'How many days   155
Since the deceiver left you here alone?'
And she replied, sighing again, 'I've spent
Ten days up until now here in this desert,
Seeing the face of no man but of you,
And yesterday of someone else, an old man,   160
Who said his son was seized a bit before
By Arabs, was a prisoner, and he
Was hurrying to Arabia to free him.
When he had heard my story, he said to me,
At Blattolivadi, five days earlier,   165
A blond boy, downy-cheeked and tall of stature,
Riding a horse and leading another after,
Was set on by Mousour, struck by his sword,
And, had the youthful Border Lord not been there,
The boy would have been killed that very instant.   170
Of all men, this, I say was my traducer,

For all the signs make certain this was he.
Alas! Alas! O wretched, hapless fate,
Thus unexpectedly deprived of good!
Before I've tasted beauty, I have lost it,   175
And like a sapling, withered ere my time!'
    "Thus spoke the girl, weeping ungovernably,
When suddenly Arabs came from the marsh,
More than a hundred of them, all with spears.
They fell on me like vultures on their food.   180
My horse in panic tore away from the branch,
But I caught up with him upon the road.
I grasped my spear, and mounted him in haste,
Then charging toward them, killed a lot of them.
Some recognizing me, said to each other,   185
'Truly, such daring and such bravery
Show it's the Border Lord. We all are lost!'
Then those who heard this fled into the marsh,
Some throwing away their spears, and some their shields,
Not hesitating for a moment even.   190
So when I saw that I was left alone,
I turned back to the fountain where the girl was.
But she had climbed into a handy tree
To watch events, and see how they came out.
But seeing me return to her alone,   195
She came down from the tree quickly to meet me,
And she entreated me, and said with tears,
'My lord and cause of my deliverance,
If you are truly he, the Border Lord,
Who rescued my belovéd one from death   200
Whose name the Arabs just now shuddered at,
Explain to me, I beg, without concealment,
If Mousour's sword-stroke really would have killed him.'
    "Astonishment possessed me, for I wondered
At seeing the girl's great passion for the boy   205
Who'd been the cause of great misfortunes to her,
Parting her from parents, stealing her wealth,
Leaving her shivering in a trackless desert

To hope for nothing but an unjust death.
And then I first learned that the love of women   210
Is warmer by a lot than that of men,
But more corruptible by lawless union.
　　"And then I said to her, 'Cease, girl, from weeping
And mourning over him whom I have saved.
I am the one who justly slew Mousour,   215
The highwayman and thief who ruled the roads
So no one dared to travel them at all.
I am the one who snatched this boy from him
And death, this boy you love, I know not why,
This unreliable boy whom you call dearest.   220
However, come, and I will lead you to him,
And I'll prepare the man to marry you,
If you'll deny the wicked Ethiops' faith.'
　　"Now when she heard this, she was filled with joy,
And answered me, 'My lord and great protector,   225
I had partaken of divine baptism
Before I joined this man, at his behest.
For, as the slave of passion, I'd no power
To resist doing everything he said.
For him I reckoned kin and parents nothing.'   230
　　"When I heard this, my friend, from the girl's lips,
It was as if a flame rose in my heart,
Offering love and an unlawful union.
At first I put aside this turbulent thought,
And wished if possible to escape this sin,   235
But fire cannot wait behind in grass.
So when I lifted her upon my horse,
And we were going to Chalkurgia,
Which is a place nearby in Syria,
I didn't know what I was doing; I burned,   240
For passion grew and utterly possessed me.
So, when we both got down to do our needs,
I filled my eyes with beauty, hands with feeling,
My lips with kisses and my ears with words,
And started doing every lawless thing.   245

And everything I wished to do I did.
Our journey was defiled with lawlessness
With help from Satan and my careless soul,
Although the girl greatly opposed the doing,
Calling on God and on her parents' souls.   250
But the great Adversary, darkness' ruler,
The foe and enemy of all our race,
Had made me ready to forget God even,
And the requital of that awful day
When all our secret faults shall be revealed;   255
When we must face the angels and all men.
    "Then, when I reached Chalkurgia at last,
We found the boy there who was her seducer,
The son of General Antiochus
Slain years ago under the yoke by Persians.   260
For when I rescued him from Mousour's hands,
I did not let him go ahead before me,
But made him known to all as a lawbreaker,
And turned him over to some friends of mine there
To stay with them until I should return.   265
    " 'If you should plan to cast this girl aside,
By Christ my Savior, you shall live no more!'
I told him not to wrong or hurt the girl,
And left him after warning him some more.
I warned him now again not to break faith,   270
But make her, as he'd vowed, his lawful wife.
I told them all how I had found the girl,
And rescued her from the Arabians.
But I passed over what was wrong to tell
Lest I should give offense to the boy's mind.   275
Then handing both of them all of the wealth
Which the girl had taken from her family,
And giving them their horses, sent them off,
Again enjoining the young man publicly
Never to do wrong to the girl again.   280
    "I went back to my wife after a little,
For April was already halfway gone,

My conscience still accusing me of sin,
Calling me a wretch for my lawless deed.
Each time I saw the sun I saw my soul,   285
And was ashamed for having greatly wronged her,
And after this I thought to change our home
Because she knew of the unlawful union.
And so we did, and moved away from there."

SIXTH BOOK

[Of Wild Beasts, Outlaws and an Amazon]

*[Basil continues his story: The month of May. He slays a
dragon and a lion that threaten his girl; then sings her a song.
He slays soldiers who demand the girl. He beats but spares
three outlaws; they plot to steal his girl. They fail, and call
on Maximo, the Amazon, for help. He beats her chief
lieutenant, her army and the outlaws; then unhorses her.
She begs to fight in single combat. He beats her, makes
love to her, and goes home, but returns and kills her. End
of Basil's story.]*

This sixth and present book of many exploits   G-vi
Records the wonders of the Border Lord
As he himself related them to friends.

    "If anyone should wish a king of months,
May surely is the king of all of them.   5
He is all earth's most pleasant ornament,
The eye of plants, the brilliance of the flowers,
The sparkling blush and beauty of the meadows.
He breathes of love, and he induces passion,
Prepares the earth to simulate the heavens   10
By decking it with roses and narcissus.
    "Now in this marvelous and pleasant month
I wished to move, alone with my fair wife,
The lovely daughter of the General.
And so when we had reached a marvelous meadow,   15
I set my tent up there, and my own bed,
Putting all sorts of growing things around it.
Tall reeds were flourishing there, and reached the top,
And in the meadow's midst cool water gushed,

Running everywhere through all the land.   20
Several kinds of birds dwelt in the grove:
There were tame peacocks, parrots too, and swans.
The parrots hung upon the branches, singing,
The swans were finding nourishment in the water,
The peacocks circled the flowers on their wings,   25
Reflecting hues of blossoms in their feathers.
But all the rest had freedom for their wings,
And played at riding on the twigs of trees.
The sparkling beauty of my noble girl
Shone brighter than the peacocks or the plants.   30
The color of her face was narcissus,
And from her cheeks a rose in bloom was dawning.
Her lips appeared a newly budding rose
Just at the time its calyx starts to open.
Curls riding very close upon her eyebrows,   35
Delights of gold, sent rays of light flashing;
In all she was indescribably cheerful.
About my bed were scents of many sweet things,
Musk, nard and ambergris, camphor and cassia;
Their odor was strong, and smelled of cheerfulness.   40
The garden had all such delightful things.
    "About the hour of noon I went to sleep
While the girl sprinkled rosewater upon me,
And nightingales and other birds were singing.
The girl was thirsty, and went to the spring,   45
And, while she wet her feet there happily,
A dragon transformed into a handsome boy
Came up to her, desiring to seduce her.
But she, knowing just what it was, remarked,
'Dragon, give up your wish. I'm not deceived.   50
My lover, who's been watching, is now sleeping'
(Then to herself she said, 'That is a dragon;
I never saw a human face like that.')
'But if he wakes and finds you, he will hurt you.'
Then shamelessly it leaped and tried to force her,   55
But crying out at once, the girl called me,

'Wake up, my master, quick! and save your darling!'
Now when her voice resounded in my heart,
I sat up quickly, saw what had distressed her
(For purposely I faced toward the spring),   60
And drawing out my sword, was at the spring,
Carried on feet that ran as swift as wings.
And when I reached the thing, it looked fantastic,
A thing fearsome to men and horribly big,
With three large heads that were ablaze with fire,   65
And were emitting flames that flashed like lightning.
And when it moved it made a sound like thunder,
So that the earth and all the trees were shaken.
Its body was heavy where the heads were joined,
Tapered behind, and thinned down to its tail;   70
It doubled up, and then stretched out again,
And charged with concentrated fury on me.
Believing what I saw was nothing much,
I raised my sword up high, and with full fury
I brought it down upon the creature's heads,   75
Getting them all. Stretched out upon the ground,
It lashed its tail about for the last time.
I wiped my sword, and put it in its scabbard,
Called to my servants who were some way off,
And ordered them to put the dragon away.   80
They did this even quicker than I tell it,
And then ran off again to their own tents.
Then I too went to bed to sleep again,
Drawn back by the sweet slumber I'd been having,
For I'd waked up from it unsatisfied.   85
The girl began to laugh hysterically
As she recalled the dragon's dreadful looks
And the quick death of its enormous bulk;
And, that she might not wake me, sought a tree
To get a little comfort after her fear,   90
When lo! a dreadful lion came from the grove,
And he too started charging towards the girl.
She cried out loudly, calling for my help,

And when I heard, I rose from bed at once.
Then when I saw the lion, I leaped quickly   95
With mace in hand, and fell on him at once,
Striking him on the head; he died right then.
When he and the dragon had been flung far off,
The girl adjured me on her soul, and said,
'Listen, master, and grant this favor to me: 100
Take up your lute, and strike a tune upon it
So I may rid my thoughts of fear of the beast.'
    "Now since I was unable to refuse her,
I struck the lute at once, and she sang to it:
    " 'I thank you, Love, who gave me my dear heart;   105
I'm glad to be his queen, afraid of no one.
He is a thriving lily, a scented apple,
And like a perfumed rose beguiles my heart.'
    "Now when the girl said 'rose' while she was singing,
I thought she held a rose between her lips,   110
Which truly seemed a rose just blossoming.
The music of the lute and the girl's voice
Sent forth a pleasant sound which the hills echoed,
Although the sound came to them from afar.
We came to know this from this evidence: 115
By chance just at that moment there passed by
Some soldiers on the road that is called Trosis,
Where, as it happened, many had been wounded,
As evident in the name the place was given.   119
These soldiers on the road had heard our songs,   123
Although a mile away, so I imagined,
And, marching from the road, they came close to us.   125
Then, seeing the much admired girl alone,
Their souls were wounded by her beauty's arrows,
And all were stirred up by unbounded passion.
Their number added up to forty-five,
And, seeing me alone, they teased with words.   130
'Give up the girl,' they said, 'and save yourself,
For otherwise you'll die for disobeying.'
They didn't know quite yet just who I was.

But suddenly the sun-born girl observed them
All fully armed, sitting upon their horses,   135
And, fearing that they meant just what they said,
She hid her face beneath a linen scarf,
And ran into my tent, quite terrified.
I said to her, 'Why don't you speak, dear?'
'Because,' she said, 'my voice died ere my soul.   140
We're being parted, and I want to die!'
'Don't think about such things, dear soul,' I said.
'Whom God hath joined, men will not put asunder!'
    "I took my mace and shield, and flew as does
An eagle from on high on partridges,   145
And every man my mace managed to touch
Was left without a bit of life within him.
But many wanted to escape. I caught them,
For no horse ever beat me in a race.
I state these things not to exalt myself,   150
But so you'll learn what the Creator's gifts are.
A few escaped me, hiding in the marshes,
And just before I put them all to death,
I captured one alive, and learned from him
Who these deranged and foolish people were,   155
And, boiling over in my rage, I spared none.
So then I tossed aside my sword and shield,
Shook down my sleeve, and went back to the girl.
    "Now when the girl saw that I had survived,
She came right out to meet me, filled with joy,   160
And with her own hands threw rosewater on me,
Kissed my right hand, and wished me a long life.
I, wishing to reproach her fear, remarked,
Though mixing words of love into my acting,
'Do I, as you do, die before I'm hurt?'   165
Aware of what I meant, she smiled sweetly,
'I saw the crowd of horsemen suddenly,'
She said, 'all armed, and you on foot alone.
And for this reason, master, fear came on me.'
We sought the tent, and kissed a thousand times.   170

I went next day down to the river to wash,
So I might change my robe, which was blood-stained,
And sent word to the girl to bring another.
  "And then I went down almost to the water,
And sat upon a tree to await the girl,   175
When lo! three handsome horsemen came in sight,
All of them wearing strangely-fashioned robes,
And keeping to the riverbank approached me,
Seeing me sitting on the roots of the tree,
And when they had come near, all greeted me.   180
They were, as later I found out from them,   120
A young and handsome outlaw, Ioannakes,
Old Philopappos, and Kinnamos the third.   122
I didn't rise for them, but remained seated.   181
'Didn't you see some soldiers near here, brother?'
I answered them without the slightest fear,
'Yes, brothers,' I said, 'I saw them yesterday,
For they desired to carry off my wife,   185
And, by God's Word, I didn't even mount—
I'll tell you later what occurred to them.'
When they heard this, they looked at one another,
And whispered, moving nothing but their lips,
'Can this be he, the Two-Blood Border Lord?   190
Well, we shall know him when we've tried him out.'
Their leader said to me, 'Can we believe
That you alone, unarmed and afoot, you say,
Have had the boldness to do battle with them?
For we have tested all of them in valor.   195
But, if you speak the truth, show it by deeds.
Pick out whichever one of us you choose,
And fight in single combat; then we'll know.'
And after smiling at them, I replied,
'If you desire, dismount, come three to one,   200
Or even, if you're not ashamed, come mounted,
And by my deeds learn who I really am.
Now, if you like, let's start the fight at once.'
Quickly I took my mace, got on my feet,

[77]

And took my shield, for these I kept with me,   205
Advanced a bit, and said, 'At your command!'
Their leader cried, 'We'll not do as you say.
Our custom's not to fight three against one;
We're bold enough for each to handle thousands.
I, whom you're listening to, am Philopappos,   210
He's Ioannakes, Kinnamos is the third.
We are ashamed to fight three against one,
So choose whichever one of us you wish.'
'All right!' I said, 'So let the first one come!'
Then Philopappos got down from his horse,   215
And lifted up his sword and shield with it,
He came at me, clearly hoping to scare me,
For truly his attack was most courageous,
And gave a sword cut squarely on my shield,
Leaving in my hand only the handle.   220
The other two were watching, and cried out,
'Another, Philopappos! Let him have it!'
But when he would have raised his sword again,
I smote him with my mace upon the head,
And if his shield had not protected it,   225
No bone in it would have been left unbroken.
But the old man dazed and much afraid,
And bellowing like a bull, sprawled on the ground.
Now when the others saw this sight, they mounted
Just as they were, and came down on me quickly,   230
Nowise ashamed, as they had boasted before.
    "Now when I saw them charge, I snatched the shield
Out of the old man's hands, and ran towards them.
There was a struggle and a stubborn battle.
Kinnamos sought to get behind unnoticed,   235
And Ioannakes struck both straight and fast.
And then I knew that they were proven fighters,
Though none of them had power to overcome me,
For each time that I shook my mace at them,
They all ran off, as if before a lion,   240
And watched me from afar, the way sheep do,

And then, like barking dogs, came back again.
And as things went like this for quite a while,
The girl caught up with me, but stood far off,
Right opposite, on purpose that I see her.   245
And when she saw them circling me like dogs,
She shot a word of help to me, and said,
'Act like a man, dear!' Straightway at this word
My strength came back, and I struck Ioannakes
Upon the right arm just above the elbow.   250
The bones were shattered, and the whole arm crushed,
And instantly his sword fell to the ground.
He went a little past me, fell from his horse,
Leaned on a rock, and held fast from the pain.

    "Now Kinnamos wished to do brave deeds alone,   255
And when he'd urged his own horse up and down,
The coward, confident he'd scare the lion,
Charged down, as if toward me, on his horse.
I struck it with my mace upon the withers,
From which blood flowed at once just like a river,   260
As well as from the charger's mouth and temples.
It fell all tangled up with Kinnamos.
Then fear took hold of him, and terror held him,
Thinking that I would hit him lying down.
But I said, 'Kinnamos, why are you trembling?   265
It's never been my way to strike the fallen.
So if you wish, stand up, and take your weapons.
We'll strike facing each other, as men should,
For flogging carcasses is just for weaklings.'
But now by signs he showed submission to me,   270
For he'd no strength to speak because of shaking.
Leaving him there, I turned around and saw
Old Philopappos coming to himself,
Shaking his head, and speaking in this fashion,
'By God, the Maker of heaven and all earth,   275
Who has adorned you with all gracious gifts,
Leave off the fighting, make an alliance with us;
We'll be your slaves if you yourself command,

Following orders, working resolutely.'
Hearing such words of friendship, I felt pity,   280
For words that are submissive calm one's anger,
And smiling at him, I said with mockery,
'You've waked; you're telling your dreams now, Philopappos.
But since you've changed in old age to contrition,
Rise, take your friends with you, go where you will.   285
Your eyes are witnesses of what occurred,
And, trust me, those you seek will miss the muster.
I want to live alone, but not to rule,
Since I'm the only child born to my parents.
It's up to you to rule, to work together   290
As well as possible, and make your raids.
But any time you wish to fight again,
Pick out anew another bunch of outlaws,
Who have not seen attempts on me, or known me,
For those who've seen what happens won't help much.'   295
    "Then Philopappos, glad to be released,
Called to advise those with him of their freedom,
For none had hoped to be judged fit to live.
Their souls were waiting at the gates of death,
But when they heard his shout, they yanked them back,   300
And, opening their mouths, gave thanks profusely,
'We've truly seen deeds which surpass all praise.
Your great good-heartedness is superhuman,
And such as none exhibits nowadays.
May God reward you, as His judgment warrants,   305
With greater favors; may you and your spouse
Live boundless years, rejoicing in each other.'
    "Then taking my belovéd in my arms,
We sat down far away beneath a tree
While the sun crossed the middle of the heaven.   310
When the three men had gone somewhere together,
Two of them, much amazed, said to each other,
For they were younger in years as well as wits:
'Really, the sight was unbelievable!
One unarmed man on foot with just a mace   315

[80]

Beat us, who were all well equipped with arms!
Us, who have routed thousands, captured cities!
Beat us completely, like some raw recruits,
Filled us with shame and cowardice and fear!
A wizard surely, genius of the place,   320
He thought our sword strokes were as good as nothing,
And in his mace was irresistible anger.
If he were human, as this world's men are,
He'd have a body and a soul, fear death,
Not challenge swords as fleshless specters would.   325
He surely was the genius of the place
To join conceitedly with us in battle!
When she appeared, you saw her infinite beauty,
Which shone more brilliantly than rays of sunlight;
We honored her as if a living image.'   330
    "This and much like it they said witlessly;
But Philopappos, as their elder, said,
'Your talk is only consolation, boys,
A story of bad luck to soothe your souls.
I myself saw a most esteemed young man   335
Who'd been enriched by all the gifts of Christ.
The man has beauty, courage, judgment, daring,
And in addition to all these, great speed.
The only consolation for us is
That no one has been found who saw the fight.   340
The name we had for valor was immense,
But since one man has beaten us, we've lost it.
However, if you want advice, my boys,
Let's not neglect avenging such an outrage,
But hasten to turn up all sorts of kinsfolk—   345
In spite of boasts, he didn't kill them all.
Then, if God wills, and if we're stationed near,
We'll fall on him at night when least expected,
And, if we catch him, gone is the distress
Which this young noble planted in our souls.   350
The girl's assigned to your name, Ioannakes.
I guess her beauty is beyond description,

[81]

For truly, never among human beings
Has beauty such as hers been seen, I take it.   355
Well, I am in my fifty-second year,
I've run through many cities, several countries,
But all were beaten like a troop of stars
Whenever the sun stretches forth his rays.
So courage, my good sir! She's yours henceforth!'   360
    "The old man spoke; they thought his speech was good,
And went up to the beacon for assembly,
And all night long brought torches for its flame,
But none of those expected came at all.
Then those who came with Philopappos said,   365
'Why give us all this trouble, brave old man?
Do you not trust us, though you've seen our courage
In deeds which you know well, and the rewards
We've had for things which we have done in war?
Have you not marveled that we were unbeaten   370
When you saw those incredible deeds of ours?
But this man's beaten us just like recruits.
As to those others, do you doubt he killed them?
But should you ask, hark to your children's counsel:
Let us give up these many fruitless toils,   375
And go to Maximo, our relative,
And beg her to cooperate with us;
She has picked troops, as you yourself must know.
Only, on no account tell her what happened,
For if she knows, she won't agree to help you.   380
Be prudent and discreet, and do this errand,
And that way we'll attract her to our plan.
And if this happens, victory is ours;
Then we shall join you when you show your torch.'
    "Now happily this counsel pleased the old man,   385
Who mounted horse, and went to Maximo.
She was descended from some Amazons
Taken by Alexander from the Brahmans.
She got tremendous vigor from her forebears,
And thought that war was the delight of life.

"When Philopappos came to her, they say,   390
He gently greeted her, and asked, 'How are you?'
She said, 'I'm well, by providence of God.
But you, O best of men, how are your children?
How is it that you came to us without them?'
Again the old man spoke, but was not truthful,   395
'My boys, both Kinnamos and Ioannakes,
Are well, with God's help, lady. They're on guard,
Keen to destroy irregulars completely.
I've been released by them to take a rest,
Or rather, as arranged by God's good will,   400
To try to find a good and precious gift.
For, as complete repose was never mine,
After my dearest children had departed,
I took to horse, and climbed up on the banks,
And watched the fords to see those who opposed us. 405
And when I reached the road that is called Trosis,
Upon the left side of the thick grown meadow,
I found loot much more valuable than gold,
A girl such as my eyes have never seen.
The brilliance of her beauty was intense,   410
And from her eyes she shed ineffable grace;
She has a young plant's stature, good to look at.
She charms all souls, just like a living image,
And is, as I have learned, Ducas's daughter.
We'd though we'd marry her to Ioannakes;   415
Another got her first, I don't know how,
And has appeared with her now in the meadow.
So if you care at all for your dear kinsman,
Bestir yourself for him, stay wide-awake,
Confirm your love, my lady, with your deeds.   420
For he who's willing to share his dear ones' grief
Is a true friend and relative indeed.'
 "Old Philopappos, chattering like this,
Made Maximo submissive in all respects,
For woman's mind is easily deceived.   425
At no time did she ask who had the girl,

But cheerfully at once told Melementzes,
Her chief Companion, leader of the others,
And smiling at him cheerfully, spoke out,
'You heard how marvelous old Philopappos   430
Has just found lovely hunting on the borders?
He asks us also to go out with him,
And share his joy and the dainty fare thereafter.
However, go out quickly, find the outlaws,
And from them all pick out a tested hundred   435
Who have good horses and the stoutest weapons,
So we'll catch anything he finds with ease.'
   "Not daring to refuse his mistress's order,
He came that very evening to the outpost,
Displayed the beacon, and collected crowds,   440
More than a thousand soldiers, all well proven.
From these he set aside a hundred nobles,
And taking these with him, went to his lady.
When she had suitably supplied their wants,
She bade them to attend in arms next day,   445
And with them started for me, filled with zeal,
While Philopappos led them eagerly.
Now when they had arrived upon the hill top,
The old man told his friends the sign arranged for,
And lit the light for those with Ioannakes.   450
The next day they were ready with the army,
And joyfully they came to Maximo,
For they were ready both as kin and allies;
And Maximo delightedly received them.
When they'd approached close to the river bank, 455
Old Philopappos thus harangued them all:
'The place, my lady and you soldiers, where
I found the girl, is very difficult.
Let's not all enter, and thus make a racket,
And so give warning to the one who guards her, 460
For, ere we come, they'll plunge into the woods
So we can't get possession of our prey,
And all our labor will be done in vain.

So, if you please, let two or three proceed,
And secretly discover where the girl is,   465
And two of us remain to watch for her.
The third will come back, tell you where she is,
And you can go with him, and not get lost.'
Then Maximo replied to the old man,
'O wise old man, I entrust command to you,   470
So do just as you wish; we'll all obey you.'
    "Then Philopappos, taking Melementzes
And Kinnamos with him, came through the river,
But ordered all the others to remain there
Until they sent some information to them.   475
At that time I was staying at my outpost,
Sitting upon a rock, holding my horse,
Keeping a constant lookout for their coming.
When Philopappos saw me, he said, 'See him?'
And pointing with his hand, showed Melementzes.   480
'He's sitting on a rock up on the ridge.
That is the man who has the girl, you know.
So let's not come upon him face to face,
But let's find out just where he keeps the girl,
And then inform the army, as was ordered,   485
For even though he is alone, he's good.
I know the sort of valor the man has,
And urge we don't appear alone against him.'
Though Kinnamos commended what he said,
Melementzes wouldn't agree at all,   490
And said, 'I cannot possibly admit
That I'd need help, even against a thousand;
Yet for one man you say to await the army?
Surely if this were said before my lady,
I would be called a craven, fearing one man.   495
I'd want to die if I were called a coward!'
With this he went for me with all his might,
Thinking the old man's words of no account,
For the barbarian race is unbelieving.
    "Now when I saw him charge, with others also,   500

[85]

For they were following to see what happened,
I took to horse, and started off to meet them.
As Melementzes came in front of all,
He held his lance out straight, so he could strike me,
But dodging it with skill as he ran past me,   505
I struck him with my mace; he fell to earth.
Then I stood watching lest he chance to rise,
And as I'd put my mind in this that moment,
I failed to see old Philopappos come,
And with a lance thrust, hurt my horse's thigh.   510
The trees were thick and very closely planted,
My horse in pain and very much excited,
And when I turned and saw the old man running,
I said to him, 'Why do you run from me?
Take me on, face to face, if you're a soldier;   515
Don't bite me like a treacherous mad dog!'
But he instead just kept on running faster,
And went with Kinnamos across the river.
So I pursued them right up to the water,
But when I saw the troops beyond, all armed,   520
I judged best not to follow without weapons,
The more so as my horse stumbled from wounds.
So I returned straight to the girl at once,
Took up my arms, changed to another horse,
And to my fair one said, 'Come quickly, dearest,   525
So I may take you to a mountain hideout.
From there you'll see our enemies destroyed,
And learn whom God has given as avenger,
And presently you'll praise His holy power.'
She got up on my horse immediately,   530
For I, of course, had furnished her provisions,
And when we reached the place of which I'd spoken,
I left her in the lookout on the hill
In which a natural cave served as her dwelling,
Hidden by trees, and very hard to find,   535
Allowing a view of what occurred far off,
But hidden so that no one could observe it.

There, as I have explained, I hid the girl,
And bade her have no fear of what might happen,
Nor to cry out at all during the melees—   540
'So that your voice won't be a guide to them,
And lead them back to you while I'm engaged,
And thereby put me into obvious danger.'
    "I rushed to the river where I'd seen their troops,
And ran along the banks to find the ford.   545
I saw that Maximo had left the others,
And with her the four greatest of the outlaws,
That is, old Philopappos, Ioannakes,
Kinnamos, and Leander, brave and proven.
They came whipping down to the river's edge,   550
Two on each side, with Maximo between,
Riding upon a charger white as milk,
Which had its mane, tail, forelock and both ears,
As well as all four of its hooves dyed red,
And all its saddlery adorned with gold;   555
Her breastplate gleamed, for it had golden edges.
She turned to the old man, and quizzed him closely,
'Tell me, who has the girl, O Philopappos?'
He said, 'That is the one,' and pointed at me.
And then she asked, 'Where are the soldiers with him?'   560
'Lady,' he said, 'he needs no one to help him,
But puts his trust in his courageous might,
And makes his way alone, and boasts of it.'
'You thrice accursed old man,' she answered him,
'You've bothered me and my troops for just one man?'   565
I boast, by God, I'll cross alone to him,
And take his head off; and I won't need you!'
    "She spoke in rage, and rushed to make the crossing,
But I said to her, 'Maximo, don't cross.
It's usual for men to come to women,   570
So I shall come to you, for that is proper.'
Then, putting rowels to my horse at once,
I dashed toward the stream, but missed the ford;
The river was high, my horse compelled to swim.

There was a channel running from the water   575
Displaying a small pool and heavy grass
In which, unfaltering and well prepared,
Stood Maximo, watching for my attack.
Some of those with her ran toward the ford,
And others hid in ambush to waylay me.   580
    "When I was sure my horse was touching bottom,
I roused him sharply; then I drew my sword,
And went for her with all my heart and skill.
But she was ready, and she ran to meet me,
And struck my breastplate with a glancing blow.   585
In no wise hurt at all, I broke her lance,
Brandished my sword again, and, sparing her,
I cut her charger's head right off with it
So that its body tumbled to the earth.
She stepped back, and she started shivering,   590
Then knelt and cried, 'Let me not die, young man!
I erred as a woman, heeding Philopappos.'
I heeded what she said, and honored her,
Pitying the great beauty which was hers,
Then left her there, and went towards the others.   595
How I prevailed I am ashamed to say
Lest you, my friend, might think I am a boaster.
For he who talks about his own exploits
Is reckoned by his listeners a braggart.
I am not boasting in revealing this,   600
I swear by Him Who gives men strength and wisdom,
For He alone is the giver of good things.
Therefore I'll tell it all as it occurred
So you who hear may show forbearance toward me.
Again I slipped into adultery's pit,   605
Because of frivolous heart and careless spirit
About which, on the whole, my tale will tell,
And it was thus, as I shall next describe:
    "Now Maximo, after she lost her horse,
Was left there on the grass, as told above,   610
And running toward the others, I'd joined battle.

[88]

Before they would attack me, they approached me,
But when they saw all those who'd fought with me
Broken upon the ground, thrown from their horses,
And recognized from these deeds who I was,   615
They trusted flight alone to give them safety;
But only a few were able to escape.
Then, when the battle ended, I turned back,
And suddenly I saw the four outlaws,
Philopappos, Leander, Kinnamos   620
And Ioannakes, coming from the woods,
Kinnamos and Leander from in front,
The old man and the other from behind.
They hoped, by putting me between, to catch me,
But all their plans were fruitless and in vain,   625
For when I saw them spurring from in front,
I disregarded those behind, and charged.
Leander didn't know me, and attacked;
I struck, and with his horse he fell to earth.
When Kinnamos saw this, he turned aside.   630
The others slung their swords around their shoulders,
And from one side they charged me with their lances.
Quickly I turned my blade around toward them,
And promptly cut the lances of them both.
They turned around in flight, and spurred their horses,   635
Not having nerve enough to look behind them.
Seeing how they behaved, I said with laughter,
'Turn back! Aren't you ashamed to fear one man?'
But they instead continued to run harder.
Pitying their defeat, I did not chase them—   640
It was my way to pity those who fled;
To conquer, not to crush; to love my foes—
So I turned back again, walking at leisure,
And coming near to Maximo, I said,
'Trusting your strength, you boasted over much!   645
Go, get together those who lived to flee,
And try your feats on those whom you can beat,
And, as you know my custom, having tried it,

[89]

Learn from what happened to you not to brag,
For God is ranged against the arrogant!'   650
    "Then she came forward so that we might meet,
Clasping her hands together gracefully,
And decorously bowed her head to the earth.
'Noblest of men,' she said, 'I must admit
Your strength's incomparable, your kindness too,   655
A thing which long ago was not held manly.
For when I was unhorsed, you could have killed me,
But spared me, for you're very great in valor.
So may the Lord preserve you, noble soldier,
My much admired master, and your dear wife   660
For many years in glory and in health.
Because I've seen a host of noble soldiers,
Warriors who were renowned and tough in battle;
But any mightier in manly deeds
I've never seen at all in my whole life.'   665
    "After she had embraced my feet, she kissed
My right hand, and then gently spoke these words,
'Blest be your father and the one who bore you,
And blest the mother's breasts which nourished you.
For such another man I've never seen.   670
And so I beg, my master, you'll fulfill
One more request, so thereby you may know
More clearly my experience in war.
Permit me to depart and mount my horse,
And in the morning I shall come to this place,   675
So we may duel when there's no one present,
And you shall learn, good sir, about my valor.'
'With pleasure, Maximo,' I said to her,
'Go where you will, and you will find me here;
Or rather, bring your other outlaws also,   680
And test them all, and learn which are the strongest.'
    "And then I caught one of the straying horses
Left by those fallen with her in the battle,
And bringing it to her, told her to mount.
    "For when her troops saw me unhorse the girl,   685

They poured around me eagerly like eagles,
Some striking at arm's length with rapid sword cuts,
Some thrusting mightily at me with lances,
And others stabbing at me with their daggers.
Who was my ally then? My guard and shelter?   690
None except God, the great and righteous Judge,
For He sent help down to me from on high,
And against expectations, kept me harmless,
Shut in the middle of so many foes,
Smitten from every side, but scorning flight.   695
For I had armor that was strongly made,
And, thanks to God, was not hurt in the battle,
And thus their boldness did not come to much,
But was extinguished quickly, with God's help.
Then with the saints, the martyred Theodores,   700
Demetrius and George, I beat them all.
I did not take a lance or bow against them,
But drew my sword, and came within arm's length.
As many of them as I caught I slew,
And earth received them when they lost their souls.   705
Others who wished to flee, I overtook,
And when they couldn't stand and fight against me,
Dismounted from their steeds, threw arms away,
Surrendered, and ran off, possessed by trembling.
Thus many of the horses were abandoned,   710
And one of these I gave to Maximo,
And crossed the river while she went towards home,
Acknowledging, I thought, much thanks to me.
   "Then, coming to my tent, I doffed my armor,
And donned a very delicate fine garment,   715
A red cap made of curly camel's hair,
Changed saddles to a star-marked chestnut horse
With disposition good for manly deeds.
I took my sword, my shield and my blue lance,
And crossed the river. It was evening now,   720
So, hesitating to approach my girl,
I sent two of her maids-in-waiting to her,

[91]

For we had several who attended us.
These had their dwelling some way from our tent,
Not all together; the men were separate,   725
And, as the women did, had their own tents,
    "Then crossing the Euphrates, as I said,
I lay down in that most delightful meadow,
Letting my horse rest while I passed the night.
Towards dawn I rose again, mounted my horse,   730
And riding to the plain, I stood there waiting.
Just as the light of day was shining through,
And the sun gleamed upon the mountain tops,
Lo, Maximo appeared upon the field.
She sat upon a well-bred mare, a black,   735
Wearing a tabard made of saffron silk,
A green turban that was sprinkled with gold.
She held a shield painted with eagles' wings,
An Arab lance, and with a sword was girded.
At once I started forward to our meeting,   740
And when we had come near, we both embraced,
Greeting each other, as was fair, in friendship;
Then spurring horses, we began the battle.
We galloped up and down for a short time,
Then charged with lances; neither was unhorsed.   745
At once we separated, drew our swords,
And fell upon each other, hitting hard.
But I forbore, good friend, from hurting her,
For it's not only a disgrace for men
To kill, but even fight at all with women.   750
But at that time she had a name for valor,
So I was not at all ashamed to fight her.
I struck her right hand just above the fingers,
The sword that she was holding fell to earth,
And she was seized by trembling and by fear.   755
    "I shouted to her, 'Fear not, Maximo!
I pity you, a woman filled with beauty.
But so you'll clearly know me by my deeds,
I'll demonstrate my strength upon your horse.'

[92]

At once I struck a downward sword stroke on   760
Her charger's loins, and cut it through the middle,
So half of it fell to one side of her;
The rest was borne to earth upon the other.
She stepped back in excessive agitation,
And in a broken voice she cried, 'Have mercy!   765
Have mercy on me, lord, who erred so badly!
Or, if you won't disdain me, let's be friends.
For I'm a virgin still, by none corrupted.
You alone won me; take your harvest from me;
You'll have me as an ally against your foes.'   770
'You won't die, Maximo,' I said to her,
'But making you my wife's impossible.
I have a lawful wife both fair and noble,
Whose love I'd never cruelly deny.
So come into the shadow of this tree,   775
And I will tell you all about myself.'
We went down to the trees beside the river,
And after Maximo had washed her hand,
And put upon the wound a proven unguent
That we are always wont to take to war,   780
She threw her tabard off, for it was hot.
Maximo's tunic was as thin as cobwebs,
And showed, as in a mirror, all her body
With breasts protruding from her chest a little.
My heart was wounded; she was beautiful.   785
When I descended from my horse, she cried,*   A 3802
'Greetings, my master!' and came running toward me,
'I am your slave indeed, by chance of war,'
And kissed me pleasantly on the right hand.   A 3805
Now as the flame of passion had been kindled,
I knew not where I was, I burned completely.
I tried in every way to escape the sin,
And I accused myself, and argued thus,

*Text in italic type is from Andros version. For explanation see note on G-vi
785-827.

For I believed it was some evil spirit: A 3810
'Spirit, why fall in love with adversaries?
Apart I have my own untroubled spring.'
While I was talking in this way, my friends,
Maximo lighted up my love still more,
Shooting her sweets words into my ears,   A 3815
For she was young and fair, a lovely virgin,
And I was wholly conquered by this sin.
So when our shame and union were fulfilled,
I left her, and I sent her on her way,
Saying these words to her for consolation,   A 3820
'Go forth in peace, my girl, and don't forget me.'
Then mounting on my horse, I crossed the river.
And after she had bathed her maidenhead,
She urged me vehemently to come back.
    "*Later, when I'd returned to my belovéd,*   A 3825
Dismounted, and had kissed her greedily,
I said, 'Behold, my soul, your own avenger,
The sort of help that the Creator gave you.'
She felt some jealousy within her heart,
And said, 'Thank you for everything, my lord.   A 3830
What burns me is why Maximo detained you;
I don't know just what you were doing with her.
God possibly knows all the hidden things,
And will forgive this sin of yours, good sir.
But, young man, see you don't do this again,   A 3835
Else God, Who judges righteousness, requite you.
So I have put all of my faith in God;
He will protect you, and will save your soul,
And grant me to enjoy your pleasant beauty
For many good years yet, my dearest heart.'   A 3840
    "*Still with persuasive words I cheated her,*
And told of Maximo's fight from the beginning,   A 3842
How I had wounded her in the right hand,   826
And added that a lot of blood was flowing   A 3844
From which Maximo might perhaps have died   A 3845
If I had not jumped off and quickly washed it,   827

[94]

Pitying her, a woman, weak in nature.
'I washed her hand, and bound the wound up well,
And that's why I was late, my scented light,   830
So none could charge that I had killed a woman.'
When I said this, the girl was much relieved,
Thinking the words I said to her were true.
   "Then, having well in mind the girl's remarks,
And boiling over in a rage myself,   835
I rode off right away, as if to hunt,
Caught up with her, and pitilessly slew her,
Adulteress, committing sordid murder.
Then I returned to where the girl was waiting,
And after we had spent a whole day there,   840
We both came down the next day to our tent
For the enjoyment of those lovely meadows.
After a day's thought and deliberation,
I thought it best to live on the Euphrates,
And built myself a bright, unusual house."   845

SEVENTH BOOK

[*Of his Life on the Euphrates*]

[*His garden and palace on the Euphrates. His father dies; his mother comes to live with him. The details of his daily life. His mother dies. Encomium on his mother.*]

Basil, the wondrous Two-Blood Border Lord,
The Cappadocians' pleasant, thriving scion,
The wreath of valor and the height of daring,
The pleasant ornament of all the young,
After bravely subduing all the borders,   5
And taking cities and unruly countries,
Chose to make his dwelling on the Euphrates.
This is the fairest river of them all,
Having its source in Paradise itself
From which it has obtained its fragrant sweetness,   10
And from its freshly melted snow its coldness.
Now from this river he diverted water,
And planted there another paradise,
A grove, strange though really pleasant to look at.
Around it was a wall of adequate height   15
With four sides under marble colonnades.
The plants inside took on a festive air,
Their branches thrived and fell on one another,
Such was the emulation of the trees.
On either side were hanging lovely vines,   20
Tall reeds were flourishing there, and reached the top,
Fruits and flowers hung one upon another,
The meadow gaily grew beneath the trees
With variegated hue and sparkling flowers,
Fragrant narcissus, roses, and with myrtles.   25

[97]

The roses were earth's crimson decoration,
And the narcissus gleamed a milky hue,
While violets sparkled with the sea's color
When it's stirred by a light breeze in a calm.
And water flowed in plenty through the meadow.   30
Several kinds of birds were dwelling there,
Some flattering human beings for their food,
But all the rest had freedom for their wings,
And played at riding on the tops of trees.
Some little birds were singing shrill sweet songs,   35
And some were clad in glory by their wings.
There were tame peacocks, parrots too, and swans.
The swans were finding nourishment in the water,
The parrots sang about the trees from branches,
The peacocks circled the flowers with their wings,   40
Reflecting in their wings the view of flowers.
   Within this wondrous pleasant paradise
The noble Border Lord put his house.
It was fair-sized, built of cut stone, four square,
With stately columns and with windows over.   45
He decorated ceilings with mosaics
Of precious marbles sparkling in their brightness,
The pavements bright with tesselated stones.
Within the house he made three upper stories
Of medium height, with decorated ceilings,   50
And cross-shaped halls with five strange cubicles,
With shining marbles that cast beams of light.
The artist had so beautified the work
That you would think you saw a tapestry
From the stones' gay and manifold appearance.   55
The floor of this he paved with stones of onyx
Polished so hard that those who saw it thought
That it was water frozen into ice.
On either hand and to the sides, he built
Long lovely banquet halls with golden roofs   60
Where he depicted triumphs of the ancients
Who'd shone in valor, all in gold mosaics.

The first was Samson's battle with the gentiles,
Rending a lion with his hands alone,
Showing the gentile city's gates and locks   65
Up on the hill when he had been imprisoned;
The mocking of the gentiles; their destruction;
Finally the temple's sudden overthrow
Accomplished by him in those days of old;
And he himself destroyed with all the gentiles.   70
And in the middle David quite unarmed,
Holding in his hand his sling and stone;
Next was Goliath, who was great in stature,
Fearful to look at, mighty in his strength,
And fenced about with iron, head to foot,   75
Holding a javelin like the beam of a loom,
Colored like iron by the painter's skill.
He painted too his actions in the battle,
And how Goliath, hit by a well-aimed stone,
Fell wounded to the earth at once; and how   80
David ran up, and lifting up his sword,
Cut off his head, and was victorious.
    Then came the fear of Saul, the meek one's flight,
Conspiracies by thousands, and God's vengeance.
    He painted too Achilles' fabled wars,   85
Agamemnon's beauty, his fateful flight;
And wise Penelope; the suitors' slaughter;
Odysseus' wondrous daring with the Cyclops;
Bellerophon slaying the dread Chimaera;
Alexander's triumph, Darius' defeat,   90
The reign of Candace, and her wisdom too,
Reaching the Brahmans, then the Amazons,
And other feats of the wise Alexander,
And many other marvelous kinds of valor:
Moses' miracles, the Egyptians' plagues,   95
Exodus of the Jews, grumbling of ingrates,
And God's vexation, and His servant's prayer,
The glorious fate of Joshua, son of Nun.
These and much else the Two-Blood had depicted

In gold mosaic in those banquet halls 100
Giving boundless pleasure to those who saw them.
There was within the courtyard of the house
A field whose length and breadth were very great
In which he put a notable work, a shrine
In the name of Theodore, saint and martyr. 105
He buried his own honored father in it,
Bringing the body there from Cappadocia,
And decorated the tomb with shining stones.
　The marvelous man then felt grief for the first time,
For when he learned that illness held his father, 110
A serious one that brought him close to death,
He hurried to the Cappadocians' country.
But coming close to his parental home,
He saw that all who came to meet him wept,
And when he learned his father had expired, 115
He tore his clothes, dismounted from his horse,
And, when he'd come inside, embraced the body,
Lamenting, and with tears he cried aloud,
"Father, arise, behold your dearest child;
Behold your only son; say some small word. 120
Counsel, advise, don't pass me by in silence!"
Then once again, raising his voice still louder,
He cried with a voice that anyone might hear,
"Will you not answer your belovéd child,
Nor speak to me in words as you were wont? 125
Alas, the God-inspired voice is still.
Alas, the mouth so sweet to all is closed.
Where is your eye's light and your body's beauty?
Who bound your hands? Who took away your strength?
Who stayed the matchless running of your feet? 130
Who dared to turn aside the boundless love
You've had for me, father? O transgression!
O utter ruin! and O bitter pain!
O with what toil and grief you gave your soul up
While calling me by name until life's end, 135
How happy had I been if for a moment

[100]

I could have heard your voice and your last prayer,
And let your soul depart while in my arms.
I would have washed your body with my own hands,
And covered up your eyes, O dearest father!   140
Now I'm the most unhappy man of all.
Immeasurable sorrow wounds my heart.
Would I had died rather than see such things!
O death, why did you grudge to me the boon
Of finding him alive, and taking me?   145
Why show yourself unjust that little time?"
With words like these the Two-Blood was lamenting,
And even made the stones lament, they say;
And mourning with him was his marvelous mother.
Thus they performed with honor the last rites   150
Upon his father's death for several days.
    The wondrous man then took his father's body,
And with his mother went to his own house,
And for a second time interred his father
Within the shrine he'd built so lovingly.   155
His mother then resided with her son.
    The things they loved so much to do thereafter
We'll tell to you, and we'll disclose a little.
They passed each day rejoicing in this way:
The wondrous man would often take his lute   160
Before the end of dinner, while the girl sang
A song surpassing that of nightingales
Or sirens in the sweetness of its sound.
And when the sound of the lute turned into dance tunes,
The lovely girl rose from her couch at once,   165
Spread silk upon the ground, and stepped upon it.
I'm quite unable to describe her movements,
The turning of her hands, her shifting feet;
These were done lightly, following the music,
While twists accompanied the striking lute.   170
But just as those who've never savored honey
Can't know its taste, this pleasure can't be told;
There was a special beauty in her style.

[101]

Then presently they'd rise up from the table,
Nourished upon delights, then to the meadow   175
Described above, in that fair paradise,
Rejoicing much, and giving thanks to God;
These noble young folks truly were admired.
One thing alone distressed their souls each day,
The unquenched dreadful flame of childlessness   180
Which only those experience who lack children.
It causes great misfortune in their lives.
They used to pray to God each day about this.
They prided themselves upon the first of virtues—
Of doing good, I mean—and charity.   185
But by God's will they failed to achieve their hope.
But, being wise, they gave great thanks to God,
And to their own faults they ascribed the blame.
    Meanwhile illness came to the Two-Blood's mother;
Within four days she laid aside her life.   190
He wept hard, and he mourned her very much.
The Two-Blood then interred her with his father.
She lived five years after her husband's death,
Delighting in all good things in the world,
And, worthy of praise, she shone among all women.   195
Once by her beauty she defeated foes,
Freed many people from captivity,
Awarded peace to cities and to towns,
And from her came the start of better things.
She put down hatred with divine assistance,   200
And everywhere brought joy and peace instead.
She bore a root and branch both fair and noble,
Who crushed the insolence of the Hagarenes,
Plundered cities and joined them to the realm.
Before the time of the noble Border Lord   205
The Ethiop tribes had entered fearlessly,
And ruthlessly destroyed the Romans' cities;
And those descended from slaves would enslave
The worthy well-born children of the free.
But when He Who was born of a Virgin for us   210

[102]

Was pleased to think it good to free us all,
He made the notable, wondrous dispensation
That foe be friend, that from Him should be born
That crown of valor, the Two-Blood Border Lord,
So there was true salvation from the foe.   215
For he has reaped a crop of such good things
That all the prisoners were paid in full,
Getting as slaves their former fearsome masters.
Then with tremendous joy their relatives
Drove these away, and took their kin again,   220
Then war in general, or rumor of war,
Was never known in his day in the least,
But everywhere was peace and quietness,
And all men constantly gave thanks to God,
And all men called the Two-Blood benefactor   225
Their great protector, and with God, their leader.
And many men delighted in his reign,
And glorified the Holy Trinity
Which should be worshipped to eternity.

EIGHTH BOOK

Of his End

[*When bathing he is taken ill. While dying he recounts his life with his girl to her. He sleeps; she thinks he is dead, and dies. He wakes, sees her lying dead, and dies. Funeral and lament of the notables. Prayer.*]

Since all the pleasures of this fickle world
Are withered in Hell, and taken by dread Charon,
Pass like a dream, and flit by like a shadow,
Dissolving all the wealth of life like smoke,
Death also took the wondrous Border Lord,   5
The cause of it occurring in the bath.
    For friends had come to see him once from Amida,
Orthodox kinsmen from his father's family,
For most, upon his father's admonition,
Had been confirmed in orthodoxy's faith,   10
And all these people eagerly desired
To see him, and to see his valor too.
And some of them, of the paternal faith,
Turned Christian too, upon his admonition.
These, as has been explained, had come to him.   15
With loving goodness he received them gladly,
And gave to them, since they were noble lords
And masters, a pleasant inn as residence,
Which was much closer to his house than others.
He spent his time with them for several days,   20
Doing extraordinary deeds of prowess,
Going out hunting with them every day.
Amazement and surprise came over them
As they observed his strength and limitless speed;

[105]

The game he found could never get away,   25
But fell into his hands, no matter what,
Whether a lion, deer, or other beast.
He had no hounds with him, nor hunting leopards,
He sat upon no horse, and used no sword,
For hands and feet alone were all to him.   30
    One day he ordered that the bath be ready
Which he had built within that paradise,
So he could bathe with friends; this was the point
At which this excellent belovéd man
Fell into a very serious illness   35
Which doctors' young assistants call lumbago.
Aware how ill he was, he left his friends,
Went to his house, and fell upon his bed,
But kept the pain and aching all to himself
In order not to grieve his precious girl.   40
But as the pain distressed him terribly,
And was acute, the girl became aware,
And, sighing deeply, said to him, "My lord,
Will you not say what pain oppresses you?
Will you not tell, dear, what your trouble is?   45
Not speaking of your pain you affect me more;
You break my heart by hiding your disease."
Yet with his moans he hurt her even more
Because he didn't want to see her grieved.
"Nothing, my soul, afflicts and crushes me   50
Except unbearable pain within my bones;
It tears apart my loins, kidneys and back,
My bones and joints; I cannot bear the pains.
Have one of the army doctors called at once."
One came the following day, and felt his pulse,   55
And from his fever knew his strength was waning,
Disease prevailing over constitution.
Then the doctor sighed and wept to himself.
The wondrous man knew that his end had come,
And saying nothing to him, bade him leave,   60
And straightway called the girl, who was within

An inner storeroom, and she ran to him.
Then, gathering his breath, and sighing deeply,
He cried, "O bitter parting from my dearest,
From joy and from all of the world's delights!   65
Sit opposite and feast your eyes on me,
For you won't see your lover any more.
I shall relate what happened from the first:
Do you remember, dear, light of my eyes,
How I was bold enough alone to seize you,   70
Not fearing your parents nor the multitude?
The army that attempted to divide us,
O my belovèd, on the darkening plain,
And how, refusing to turn back, I slew them?
And how I cast your brothers from their horses,   75
Wholly unhurt, obeying your injunction?
Remember how I chose to take just you,
But left your dowry to your father for life?
It was entirely for love of you, dear;
I did all this to win you utterly.   80
Do you remember, dear, Blattolivadi,
And how the dragon found you at the spring,
And how the shameless brute tried to seduce you?
And you cried out, and called on me for help,
And how I heard, and quickly came to the spring,   85
Where, thinking nothing of this apparition,
I cut the heads off that were flaming fire?
I dared to do these things for love of you;
I would have died rather than have you sigh.
Remember too the lion in that meadow   90
Which, while I was asleep, my scented light,
Sprang to tear you apart. You gave a cry,
And when I heard, I leaped toward him quickly,
And killing him, delivered you unhurt,
My dearest, from his claws, but filled with terror?   95
Then, when I would divert you with my lute,
The outlaws, Ioannakes' men, guided
By your singing, came shamelessly toward us,

[107]

And daringly attempted to divide us.
You know, my soul, what happened to them then: 100
Without sleep, I delivered them to death.
These things I did because of love for you,
Preferring not the world, or even life.
Do you remember, dear, the wondrous outlaws,
Philopappos, Kinnamos, Ioannakes,   105
Renowned for valor, everywhere extolled,
And how they met me unarmed at the river,
All three of them on horses, fully armed?
You know how eagerly they tried to kill me?
When they observed you coming out before me?   110
But you cried out to me, and helped by saying,
'Be a man, dear, so they won't separate us!'
How, strengthened much by this, I routed them,
Beat them full force, and wounded with my mace,
And then, abashed by words, granted them life?   115
These things I did from my excessive love
For you, my darling, so that I might win you.
How I unhorsed Maximo, killed those with her,
And then, persuaded by your words, ran back,
And slew her secretly, without your knowledge?   120
And many other things I did for love
Of you, my soul, to win you utterly.
But I have missed my mark, and lost my hope,
For be assured, I certainly am dying,
And Charon the invincible defeats me.   125
Hell parts me from my love for you, my dear,
And the tomb covers me and the great pain
And grief I can't bear for your widowhood.
But how shall I bewail your grief, belovèd?
How comfort you? Where leave you, now a stranger?   130
What mother will weep for you? What father pity?
What brother watch, now that you are not cared for?
But, O my dearest, mark these words of mine,
And do not disregard my final wish
That you may live henceforth afraid of none.   135

I know you'll not endure your widowhood,
So take another husband when I'm dead,
For youth will certainly compel you to it.
See that you're not misled by wealth or fame,
But take a boy who's brave and bold and noble,   140
And as before, you'll reign on earth, my dear."
He said these words with tears, and ceased from speaking.
And from her heart the girl sighed bitterly,
And warm tears raining down her cheek, she spoke.
"My lord," she said, "I place my hope in God   145
And in the chaste and stainless Mother of God.
Until I die, no one but you shall know me,
And He'll redeem you soon from your dread sickness."
She spoke, and went into an inner storeroom,
And stretching hands and eyes toward the east,   150
And raining many tears upon the floor,
She offered prayer to God Most High as follows:
"O Lord God, Thou Who hast built the ages,
Hast made the heavens firm, and founded earth,
And by Thy Word put all seen things in order,   155
Who with Thy hand hast formed man out of clay,
Who out of nothing brought all things to being,
Hear Thou my prayer, unworthy as I am,
See Thou my humbleness, see my affliction,
And as Thou raised the lame in pity once,   160
And the centurion's little daughter once,
And Lazarus, dead four days, from the tomb,
So, even now raise up a youth despaired of,
In Thy goodness, pity my own compassion,
Christ, have compassion on Thy servant's youth,   165
Although we've sinned before Thee much, O Word,
And are wholly unworthy of Thy mercy.
But Thou art merciful; receive the prayer
Of one in pain, raise up this youth despaired of,
Nor overlook my tears, the joy of angels.   170
Benevolent God, have mercy on my exile,
Pity my loneliness, and raise him up.

[109]

If Thou wilt not, almighty God, then order
That I die first, give up the ghost before him.
Let me not see him stretched out dead and silent, 175
Nor see the hands which know such manly deeds
Bound crosswise and remaining motionless,
Eyes covered up, and feet wrapped up together.
Do not permit me to see such affliction,
O God, my Maker, Who canst do all things!" 180
   Thus with a broken heart, the girl was praying,
When, looking at the Border Lord, she saw
That he was silent, yielding up his soul.
Unable to endure this infinite grief
And measureless despondency, she fell 185
Upon the youth in sympathy, and died.
She'd never had experience of grief,
And therefore was not able to endure it.
He noticed then, and touched her by the hand—
By God's compassion he was still alive— 190
And seeing her incredibly thus dying,
He said, "Praise God, Who ordereth all things!
My soul won't have the unendurable pain
Of leaving her alone here, now a stranger!"
Putting his hands crosswise, the noble youth 195
Delivered up his soul to the Lord's angels,
And both the illustrious young people's lives
Ended at one time, as if by agreement.
   Now when the boy cupbearer saw their death,
He told the household table servant at once 200
With tears and wailing; these told those outside;
And presently the news was spread abroad.
Then many rulers from the East arrived:
Charzianians and Cappadocians,
Buccellariots, Podandites, Tarsites, 205
Mavronites, Baghdadis, Bathyrryakites,
Nobles from Babylon and from Amida
Rushed to attend the Border Lord's interment.
The crowd that was assembled was so big

[110]

That all the court outside the house was filled.   210
    Who has the power to tell their lamentations?
Their tears, their cries, the number of their sorrows?
For all became beside themselves with grief,
And tore their hair, and plucked their beards, and cried,
"Let the earth quake, and all the world lament.   215
O sun, be darkened and conceal your beams.
Be blackened, moon; no longer show your torch;
And all the beacons of the stars be quenched.
For that bright star that shone throughout the world,
Basil the Two-Blood, ornament of young men,   220
And his own spouse, the glory of all women,
Sank suddenly from the world at the same time.
Come, all your friends and lovers of true valor,
Mourn for the noble, daring Border Lord.
Lament him who was fearsome to all men,   225
And who has vanquished every adversary,
And has brought peace and deep tranquility.
Come hither, women, weep for your own beauty,
You who boast of beauty and trust in youth,
Mourn for the beautiful and most chaste girl.   230
Alas, what do we see? Behold, two lights
Which lit the world, and set before their time!"
This and the like was said in lamentation
By those at the interment of the bodies.
    Now when the funeral hymns had all been sung,   235
And all things in the house given to the poor,
And the remains were buried in the tomb,
They set up monuments to them in a pass
Near by a certain place that is called Trosis.
The Border Lord's tomb, standing upon an arch,   240
Is made of porphyry so those who see it
From the outside may bless the fair young couple.
The mountain ridge is visible from afar.
(Things in a high place can be seen far off.)
Then all who had assembled there went up,   245
The notables, the rulers, all then present,

[111]

And put wreaths on the tomb, and circled it,
And weeping tears ungovernably, said
"Behold, low lies the very heart of valor!
Behold, low lies the Two-Blood Border Lord,   250
His parents' crown, the glory of all youth!
Behold, low lies the flower of the Romans,
The boast of emperors, the splendor of lords,
The dread of lions and of all wild beasts!
Alas! Alas! What happened to such valor?   255
O God, where is his might, and where his courage?
Where the unequaled fear his name produced?
For at the Two-Blood Border Lord's mere name
Shuddering fear and cowardice seized all
Because the youth received from God such grace   260
That just his name would rout his enemies.
Thus, when this wondrous man went out to hunt,
All of the beasts would run down into the marsh.
But now he's mastered by a little tomb,
And looks to all both powerless and idle.   265
Who was so bold he dared to bind the strong?
Who was so strong he conquered the unbeaten?
Vindictive Death, accessory to all ills,
Thrice-curséd Charon, joint destroyer of all,
Insatiate Hell, three murderers of men,   270
These three, unpitying to every age,
Wither all beauty and destroy all glory.
They spare not young men, nor respect the old,
Nor fear the strong, nor honor give the rich;
Beauty they pity not, but make it dust.   275
They turn all things to clay and stinking ashes.
These have now seized the wondrous Border Lord;
The tomb is master and earth withers him.
His lovely flesh, alas, the worms consume,
And Hell is shriveling his snowy flesh.   280
Through what occasion did this come upon us?
Through Adam's disobedience and God's judgment.
But, O my God and Master, such a soldier,

[112]

So young, so lovely, and so sweet to all!
Why let him die, and not live for all time?   285
'There shall be none who live,' said God the Father,
'And not see death, for life is transitory;
Things seen are transitory, glory is vain.'
Christ, who in all the world like this has died?
The flower of youth, the glory of the brave.   290
Christ, let him live again, and bring his spirit,
And let us see him carrying his mace;
Then let us die at once, and none remain.
Woe to all good things in this erring world,
Woe to delight, to joy, and to all youth,   295
Alas for those who sin without repenting,
And those who trust in youth, or boast of strength!"
When they had mourned in this and similar ways,
Those who had gathered for the burial
Of those untainted bodies, left for home.   300
   But Christ, Almighty King, Maker of all things,
Save noble Basil, well-belovéd scion,
And with him save his lovely blooming spouse,
And all who love to live in orthodoxy.
And when Thou sittest on earth to judge men's souls,   305
Then, O my Christ, protect and save them harmless,
And range them on Thy right hand with Thy sheep.
To us, who have received our life from Thee,
Give strength, protect us from our adversaries,
So we may praise Thy undefiled great name,   310
The Father's and the Son's and Holy Spirit's,
The Trinity's, one nature, unconfounded,
For long and infinite ages upon ages.

THE END

FROM THE ANDROS VERSION
1] [*The Story of Basil's Mother*]

From Eustathius to a certain Manuel, his dearest friend

Ten Books
about
THE TWO-BLOOD
BORDER LORD
and his parents

My dearest and my best beloved boy
You've often urged me to set forth for you
The Two-Blood Border Lord's exploits in writing,
So, when I heard your message, I felt shamed,
And started out at once to write for you   5
All of the deeds and all the marvelous things
Accomplished by the Two-Blood and his parents;
And so I shall begin the story thus:
  Basil the Two-Blood was a border lord
From Cappadocia, born, let all men hear,   10
Of certain parents, and of Christian forebears,
Well-bred and beautiful, and very rich,
Of royal race, well known to everyone.
One part was Anatolian and Roman,
And lived in Cappadocia from the first;   15
And one from Syria, that lovely country.
  Now from these wonderful, courageous lords
A certain marvelous king sprang up amongst them;
Both bold and daring, he was rich from birth,
And, to his credit, from the Ducas clan.   20
As to his name, and may I say it clearly,
He'd been called Aaron in the Syrian tongue

But now was called Andronicus in Greek.
  So this most marvelous and handsome king
Became beloved by all, both God and men.
Just, irreproachable and firm, but guileless,
He lived by God's law only with his wife,
She being from a clan of Christian parents
Of royal race; they were the Magastrani.
Again, as to her name, she was called Anna.
  These parents also brought forth children, boys,
Contented, thriving, all five filled with courage.
But still the parents' souls and hearts were pricked
As by a sword's point since they lacked a girl.
For long they prayed to God and to the Saints.
Then waited patiently for God to give
A lovely girl in answer to their prayers.
He hearkened to their prayers, moreover, too;
And then the queen conceived within her womb
A girl this time, a most amazing child.
  The king immediately called a seer
To tell if this were true, and to disclose
Whether it was a girl the queen was bearing.
The seer was very wise and wonderful,
And told the king the whole truth right away:
  "Most admirable, noble, handsome king,
The queen, your wife, conceived a little child
Upon whose birth you will take great delight,
For truly, it's a girl; so says the omen.
On this account take heed that when the girl
Is twelve years old she doesn't fall in love.
  "For an Emir will take her as his wife,
Snatching her from her brothers and her parents,
But he'll become a Christian after that.
So you must build a marvelous palace for her,
All fresh and cool and bright, filled with delights,
And put your daughter in this lovely place
So that her thoughts may not incline to love."
  Now when the course of nine months' pregnancy

25

30

35

40

42

44

45

50

55

60

Had finally reached the end, a girl was born, 61
Most beautiful and thriving, white as snow. 63
And then, of course, the king was filled with joy.
The queen rejoiced with him, with all the people, 65
Both lords and satraps, and the common folks.
  Baptized in water from the holy font,
The girl was christened Irene by her parents,
And brought up all her days as it was proper
Both by her nurses and her gentlewomen, 70
And shone like sunlight in their shining eyes.
  When she had reached the age of seven years,
The king himself began to worry greatly
About the proper guarding of his daughter
Lest from some whim she might incline toward love, 75
And then succumb to death from passion's sickness.
  So, on a site both airy, fair and charming,
Where there were fresh trees, frosty, snow-white springs,
A dewy place with fountains of delight,
Where nightingales cast spells, and swallows sang, 80
The king gave orders to erect a palace,
And built a wondrous big one of three stories.
And in that splendid palace which he built,
They shut the maiden up with many tears
To keep her out of range of passion's sickness, 85
  To stay with her they gave three nurses to her,
A dozen gentlewomen, fifty slave girls,
And told her nurses she must learn her letters
To keep her mind from scattering every way.
  He gave three thousand Saracens, old soldiers, 90
To keep watch at the gates on every side,
So that love's arrow might not find an entrance
To wound her heart and launch her into passion.
And to the huge extent of that great palace
They put one tiny gate with an iron lock, 95
Which all himself, the king would always lock,
Closing it all himself, and sealing it.
  Within he planned and built an inner garden

At which, I think, if you should spy it out,
Your mind would marvel and your sense be stunned. 100
[And there he built a marvelous big pond.] 100a
On every side that pond was furnished with 101
Peacocks and partridges made out of silver,
And cranes and parrots, swans and turtle doves. 103
Each of the birds was singing its own song, 105
And on one side some living birds were singing,
And these mechanical, insentient birds
Were rivalling the sentient, living ones,
Together singing songs that were vivacious,
And, by their melody, refreshed the heart. 110
   The pond had in its midst twelve little islands,
And on each island grew one kind of tree,
And each of these had charms all of its own.
   They built a bath for her within the garden;
You'd marvel at the workings of this bath. 115
The basin for the bath they made of bronze,
And outside of the palace built a furnace,
Put up a big pipe made wholly of bronze,
Which came into the bath out of the furnace,
And flame rose up out of the pipe of bronze 120
So heat kept bubbling up within the basin. 121
The water rose from some contrivance also. 104
Truly, the king wished she might never have 122
A love that came from mere infatuation.
   The maiden finally reached the age of twelve,
The age the seer had prophesied for her, 125
And in her beauty she excelled the moon,
And had the lovely stature of a cypress.
She stifled love; her manner of affection
Appeared as if it never had been changed,
And only play and smiles were deemed important, 130
And thus her wandering was observed too late,
For she was found first one place, then another.
   Her face was bright and crystal clear and white;
She blushed a bit, enough to make her rosy.

Her eyes were somewhat darkish when she smiled,   135
But dripped with passion when she opened them,
Filled with the sweetness of the charms of love,
And always were surrendered up to passion.
    The quickness that she had in coquetry
Revealed the passionate nature of her love,   140
And deep within her dwelt the bow of Cupid
With which she shot each young man in the heart,
Because her form was fair and shone like sunlight,
So if one stared at her and looked her over,
It stole his reason and his very senses;   145
He looked at once a soulless, senseless corpse.
    Her eyelids were amazing, as if painted;
She had a lovely head, and hair so long
Its length was even greater than her stature.
Her lips were full and had been tinted red,   150
And were surrendered for a kiss of passion.
A fountain full of charms was dripping from them.
Her face was rounded with a lovely chin,
And pearly teeth; she was a child of charms.
Her neck was middle sized, as were her limbs.   155
These were the gifts of grace that maiden had,
And who can count the other things like these?
    Before she'd had a lesson in love's charms,
She saw that Cupid's bow was all around her,
And, until later, thought it very evil.   160
She also saw his portraits and admired them,
Thinking the painted Cupid like a child,
Pink, young and tender; he looked like an apple,
And held a mighty bow drawn strongly back.
He aimed his arrow at a youth, and shot;   165
And that poor youth was standing there and waiting;
His breast was bare, the arrow in his heart.
    She wondered too why Love was wearing wings,
And to her nurses and her women said,
"Who is this person, frightful, fearsome, great,   170
Mighty and powerful, and huge to look at,

With fire and bow and arrows in his hands,
Inkstand and paper? Does he wish to write
While dragging men and women by the neck,
Though holding lovely girls like turtle doves?   175
He's fearsome, and is very much the master,
Bold as a lion, cruel, wild, bloodthirsty,
And has enormous power over men."
    Then one among her nurses quickly said,
"He whom you see, miss, whom you think you admire,   180
Is very powerful and very fearsome.
Heartbreaking Love is what all people call him,
And none has yet escaped his flaming bow,
For great and small, he makes them threefold slaves.
If one escapes, Love comes upon swift wings,   185
Throws fire and thunderbolts into his heart,
Then, shooting it, he casts him into Hell.
But when Love's blind, and so he often seems,
He ties him up, enslaves him, makes him poor,
Writes on a card that he's a threefold slave,   190
A slave of one enslaved, thus thrice enslaved.
Whoever else falls to his hand meets him,
Loses his sense at once; his life is ruined."
    Now when the yearning maiden heard these words,
She laughed with longing, and said to her nurse,   195
"I don't myself fear mighty Love at all,
Though he bear flames or have a lion's strength."
    The sun went down, and then the evening came.
The girl went to her room and went to sleep,
And then that awesome Love made war against her.   200
He shot his arrow at her, lit a flame,
Wounded her heart, and set it all afire.
And while she slept, he said to her in anger,
"Tell me, how dared you look upon my face
So boldly that you never even shuddered?   205
Why did you not fall at my feet and beg?
I've put you in my book, my list of slaves;
I wrote you down to be a threefold slave,

[120]

And placed you first compared with those your age.
You fool! You wished to run away from Love   210
To some place in this world he dares not go?
Did you not grieve, girl, or know what he is?
Did not your heart ache? Did you not burn up?
    "I sympathize with you, grieve for your beauty.
You shall not wither ere your time from love.   215
I'll bring you up myself and teach you love,
And if you run away, I've wings to catch you.
You see my flames; they are to burn you up.
You see my arrows; they're to shoot you down.
If you're a disobedient slave, or would be,   220
I'll call my executioner to take you,
So you may learn the pestilence of longing."
    So spoke the thief of souls, Love, as she slept,
Then flapped his wings at once, made a big din,
Which terrified the girl, then journeyed on.   225
The maiden in her fright woke up at once,
And all her nurses ran hurrying to her.
Her gentlewomen came and gathered around her,
And then she told that frightful thing, her dream.
    After she'd told her tale, and fear was gone,   230
The girl went to the painted Love she saw,
And begged and worshipped, kissed it countless times,
And sighed and wept, and then she said to it,
    "Love, fearsome sovereign wearing golden wings,
You have tremendous power to pull our heartstrings.   235
I tremble at your rule, I fear your wrath,
And simply can't endure your awesome power.
I beg you now that you will pardon me,
And pardon that by which I have offended.
Don't punish me for what I seemed to think.   240
It was from ignorance and foolishness
That I disdained you, Lord and Emperor.
I never thought that you would treat me thus;
That's why I spoke to you this thoughtless way.
If I offended you, pardon me, Love!   245

[121]

You scared me first; have mercy on me now!
I am your slave completely, please believe it!"
    There were the words the maiden uttered then
To Love the terrible, and others like them.
    She didn't know what her great love would come to;   250
She had the flame, desire; the spark, affection;
This mighty fire was scattering her thoughts
To handsome men grown bold, who seemed like heroes;
She looked on them as lovely precious stones.
The coquetry and dances that she tried   255
Ruled over throne and mirror in her chamber.
She sat upon her throne, looked in the mirror
While she adorned the beauty of her face.
Her eyes were suns, her eyebrows crescent moons,
Her beauty lovely, whiter than the snow.   260

Who's seen this girl so slender,   so flower-like and tender?
Each evening she shone,   a glittering precious stone.
Who has the grace to be   a pearl as white as she?
To stand and gaze with love,   pure as a turtle dove,
On brave young men, and choose   which precious stone to use?   265
Since she was young and tender,   just twelve years old and slender,
Grown very brave and fair,   although she's pure as air,
And then puff up and fight,   a lion in her might,
Those with the amorous eyes,   the strong young men she spies.
This was that lovely maiden   with charm and beauty laden,   270
Brought up within a cage,   a bird of tender age.
    Thus far is about her raising;   and yes it is amazing.
But then the girl began   to call and talk to a man
Whose tender looks were those   of a fresh and lovely rose,
So slim and tall that he   was like a cypress tree.   275
Apart he kept his love   just like a turtle dove,
And held a steadfast view   on joy in marriage too.
    The first book's ended there,   but we have kept the air
        To sing the second book about the wedding.

Outline of the Second Part,
The Book of the Border Lord's Mother

Book Two's about the Border Lord's Mother:
How the Emir kidnaped her from her parents,
And how the maiden's brothers joined in battle,
Beat the Emir, took him as brother-in-law,
And went back to their house, and held the wedding.

SECOND BOOK OF THE BORDER LORD

When finally they had been joined in wedlock,   285
That very beautiful and lovely maiden
Disclosed the passion which she'd held in check,
And how she'd been consumed by flames of love,
The usual kind that women feel for men.
Her father'd gone upon some expedition   290
In order to collect his exiled army.
She'd begged her mother's leave to quit the house
And take a little stroll, the maiden said.
Her mother listened to her daughter's plea,
And hitching horses to a four-wheeled carriage,   295
And putting drinks and dainties in the carriage,
Sent her with all the nurses that she had,
Choice slave girls and her gentlewomen too.
These her belovéd daughter took along.
And then the maiden walked to a marvelous place.   300

.   .   .   .

[*At this point the Andros version merges into the story as
it is told in the Grottaferrata version, although there is no
point at which the transition can be made smoothly.*]

2] [*A Visit with Philopappos*]

And when they came together to the house,   1566
They ate and drank, rejoicing every day.
His father, the Emir, after those years
Which, with the sun, ran circling through the heavens,
Passed his time studying the ways of the Lord,   1570
And every day rejoicing with his wife,
Together with his sons and all his friends,
Until he reached the portal of old age,
Leaving all deeds of valor to his son.
   Now when the handsome, noble Two-Blood came   1575
Himself up to the measure of his manhood,
And became a proper man among men,
He rose one day, and leaped upon his horse,
Picked up his lance, and grabbed hold of his mace,
And gathering the people, took his own men,   1580
And, as with toil they went along the street,
They heard a lot about the valorous outlaws
Who hold the passes and do manly deed,
And the desire came over him to know them.
So, going off alone, he found a reed bed,   1585
And saw a fearful lion spread out, flayed
By Ioannakes' hands, that marvelous man.
The Two-Blood Border Lord observed the lion,
Sighed from the bottom of his soul, and said,
"When will you see those brave men, eyes of mine?"   1590
   And then he found the outlaws' water boy,
And questioned him at length about the outlaws.
The water boy muttered this to the Two-Blood:
"My good young man, why do you want the outlaws?"
And to the water boy he answered this: 1595
"I wish myself to be one of the outlaws."
So then he took the Two-Blood, and they went
Into the brigands' strange and fearful den.
   And there lay Philopappos on a bed

[124]

With skins of many beasts strewn up and down it.   1600
Then Basil the young Border Lord bowed down,
Paid his respects to him, and greeted him.
Old Philopappos thus replied to him,
"Welcome, young man, if you will not betray us."
Then Basil thus replied to him in turn,   1605
"I am no traitor. No, I seek to be
An outlaw here and now in camp with you."
And when the old man heard, he answered thus,
"If you would boast you want to be an outlaw,
Just take this club, and go below on guard.   1610
Then, if you're able to fast fifteen days,
And do not let sleep close the lids of your eyes,
And after that go off and slaughter lions;
And if you bring the skins of them all here,
And if again you can go back on guard   1615
When princes with a host of people pass,
With bride and groom, if you can go amongst them,
And seize the new bride, and then bring her here,   1619
Then, if you please, you may become an outlaw."   1620
   Now when the Two-Blood heard, he answered thus:
"Don't talk of that ! I did that as a child.
I'll only tell you this, brave Philopappos:
I'll catch a hare upon an uphill slope,
Or stretch myself to catch a flying partridge."   1625
   And then old Philopappos told his outlaws
To bring a silver chair. The Two-Blood sat.
They set a marvelous table out before him,
And all both ate and drank most pleasantly.
And after that each one of them kept saying   1630
That he could beat a lot of valiant men.
Then Philopappos asked the Border Lord,
"And you, young man; how many can you thrash?"
And Basil answered quickly in this way:
"Come, boys, and let us all take quarterstaves,   1635
And let us all go off to where it's level,
And all play quarterstaff with one another,

[125]

And he who wins shall take the other's staff."
   Then all of them took up their quarterstaves,
Great Kinnamos as well as Ioannakes,   1640
The Two-Blood too, as well as most of the others,
And all of them went down where it was level,
And played at quarterstaff with one another.
   And then that Basil, he who was the Two-Blood,
Took up his staff, and went right in amidst them,   1645
Struck some with his staff, and others with his knuckles,
And when the hands of those brave men grew slack,
The Two-Blood picked up all their quarterstaves,
And going to the old man, said to him,
   "Accept your outlaws' staves, O Philopappos.   1650
If you're displeased, I'll do the same to you!"
   When he'd accomplished this, the Border Lord
Returned to the road where all his people were,
And after that they all went to their dwellings.
So all his days the Two-Blood kept rejoicing,   1655
That marvelous Basil, glory of the brave,
And all kept shuddering for him in his battles.   1657

[The outline of the fifth book is omitted]

   And now, dear friend, I'll tell you this as well: 1665
Just at that time, that handsome man named Ducas,
The General of part of Romania
Had a fair daughter who was named Eudocia,
Whose name the Border Lord was always hearing,
For she was beautiful and nobly bred.   1670
   And so one day he leaped upon his horse,
Took his Companions with him, and went hunting,
And when they'd hunted, they were going home.

   *[This scene leads into the wooing which commences at G-iv
254.]*

3] [*The Blinded Cook*]

Nobody ever dared stand near his tent,   2322
And even his brave men would not stand near him.
The Border Lord became so terrible
That just the sight of him created fear,   2325
One day a cook replied to him too sharply;
He slapped the wretched man upon the face
So hard the fellow's eyes at once fell out.
He was dismissed, and stayed away till buried.
Thereafter he announced none should come near him   2330
With the exception of his noble girl
In whom he took great pleasure all his life.

4] [*The Story of Ancylas*]

"I am an only son and live alone.   3066
Since I began to fight I've not gone out
On even one exploit, except one day
When, mounting my horse, I went out to the plain.
I met a youth in Mesopotamia,   3070
Handsome and capable, and very brave.
I liked his charger, and I wished to have it.
My eye was on his horse, and his on me—
And he was very handsome, very brave.
Boasting a little he gave me a mace blow,   3075
And after that he took my mace away,
And wrote a letter on it all in blood,
And this is the beginning of his message,
'O Border Lord, don't grieve or fret your heart.
The lion named Ancylas is out of reach.   3080
I came for you; I had no other task.
I've finished. Finish praying, Border Lord.
You'd best explain to all the outlaws thus:

[127]

"It was a mighty blow Ancylas gave me,
And though a valiant man, he didn't kill me." ' 3085
  "This was the wonderful Ancylas' letter,
So I went up to him, and took it from him.
And now I wish to tell what happened to him.
I jumped up, mounted, and I grasped my mace,
And in great pain I went off to my tent, 3090
Threw stirrups off, dismounted from my horse,
And read the letter in blood upon my mace.
I planned at all times that I'd pay him off.
I finished out the time while pain was dragging,
And when this hostile time had been completed, 3095
I figured to myself that I'd repay him
The debt I owed him for both blow and letter,
That marvelous and very brave Ancylas
Whom they are always trusting with exploits.
I took my lute, and with it took my shield, 3100
Untied my mace, and went to see Ancylas.
And when I had come near Ancylas' house,
I struck my lute, and then began to sing,
Pleasantly chattering, astounding all,
And the beginning of my song was this: 3105
'In these ravines and in these mountain passes
And rocky places, noble men rejoice
In manly blows; the brave rejoice still more.
One time one lent a manly blow to me,
And I admit the debt, just as he wished, 3110
And want to make repayment that is fair,
So I've come back, and shall repay him this.'
  "Now when Ancylas heard the words I sang,
With the audacity that was his habit,
He urged his little horse, and charged down on me. 3115
I spurred my mount, and then began to strike him,
And tapped him with my mace upon the forehead.
He fell down from his charger and lay silent.
So I dismounted, grasped him to arouse him,
When with a groan the youth at once expired." 3120

[128]

5] [*Beginning of the Escorial Version*]

E

"Let noise and blows and threats not frighten you.
Do not fear death more than your mother's curse.
Beware a mother's curse, not blows and pains.
If they should tear you limb from limb, see that you do
        no shameful thing
If we dismount.   5
Let them kill all five us; then let's take her.
Attack the Emir's audacity with a will,
And guard both hands so God may give us help."
   Then the Emir mounted and came at him.
He rode upon a star-marked, dappled charger   10
Which had a golden star upon its forehead,
And all four of its hooves were shod with silver—
It had been shod with nails of solid silver.
Its tail was perfumed with the scent of pearl,
A red and green eagle on back of the saddle,   15
His breastplate glittered in the rays of sunlight,
The lance he wielded was of blue and gold.

6] [*Defeat of the Emperor Basil*]

Sb

48   There was a certain emperor named Basil who, on learning of the exploits and brave deeds of Devgeny, became exceedingly angry with him, and sought by every means to catch him. The Emperor Basil was guarding all the land of Cappadocia, and sent Devgeny messengers with a letter that was all lies and flattery. The little confection he wrote was as follows: "Brave Devgeny, I have a great desire to meet you. Therefore will you please come before my majesty today, because your courage and your exploits have become renowned in the whole world, and for this reason I have a great longing to see your handsome face."

49   So they brought the emperor's letter to Devgeny, and Devgeny read it, and realized that it was deceptive. Then he answered the emperor: "I am of humble descent, and your majesty has no traffic with me. But if you wish to meet me, take only a few soldiers with you, and try not to make me angry, because youth incites a man to do many foolish things. If I become angry, I shall exterminate your army, and you will not return still safe and unharmed."

50   The messengers returned, and conveyed to the emperor what Devgeny had said. The emperor was very angry, and at once gave orders for them to reply to Devgeny: "My child, I do not desire to bring many warriors with me, but I feel a desire to look upon your youthfulness. My majesty has no other evil intention in mind." The messengers arrived and conveyed the imperial message to Devgeny, and then Devgeny answered: "Tell the emperor: 'I do not fear your majesty, nor your many warriors, because I put my faith in God. I do not fear your plans, and if you wish, come to the river Euphrates where we may meet. However, if you come with numerous troops, it will not go well with your majesty, and I shall destroy your troops.'"

51   Then the messenger came to the Emperor Basil, and communicated Devgeny's message to him. The emperor collected his troops and put them in order, and after this he went to the place Devgeny had specified on the Euphrates River, where he pitched his tents not far from the river. The imperial tent was very big, bright red, and its top was pure gold. On the inside his tent was big enough for many thousands of warriors. All his soldiers were there, some in the tent, and others in a concealed place.

52   The emperor waited beside the river six days, and said to his generals: "Do you think Devgeny has been informed of our arrival, and plans nothing against us? Or does he intend to come with a big army?" As soon as the Emperor Basil pronounced these words, he was frightened, because Devgeny sent his messenger to the emperor to say: "It makes an impression on me that the emperor is pleased to come because of me, who am unworthy. I have explained my character, and now I see that you have collected a big army, and wish to make me worship you. That, however, is a disgrace to me, because my reputation has spread to all the earth, and to all countries. So now, if you can, do that which you had in mind to do."

53   And the Emperor Basil said: "What effrontery you have towards my majesty that you will not submit." And he sent his messenger with his message across the river. And Devgeny received the emperor's messenger, and learned from him the message that the emperor had sent. And again Devgeny replied: "Say to your lord these words: 'If you put your faith in your great power, I myself have put my faith in God, my Creator. Your power cannot be compared with the power of God. But time is passing. Make ready for war early tomorrow, and come with your great power, and see how the courage of one humble man stands up to you. Because I hate to . . .'" The messenger returned, and told the emperor Devgeny's words, and the emperor called his leaders at once, and held a council. His leaders said: "For what reason are you emperor, since just one lone man makes you afraid? We don't see any troops with him."

54   Devgeny's envoy crossed the river quickly, and told Devgeny what had happened at the emperor's council. And the following

day, very early, the Emperor Basil was in array for battle, and was holding a consultation about crossing the river, having in mind to catch Devgeny like a hare in a net. Devgeny, seeing the large number of the Emperor's Basil's troops, understood that the emperor intended to cross the river in order to strike him. Then he become beside himself, and said to his companions: "Come look for me in a little when I shall have attended to the emperor!"

55 So saying, he leaned on his lance, and then gave a leap, and like a fearsome hawk he found himself on the opposite side of the river, and cried with a loud voice: "Where is the Emperor Basil who wishes to do battle with me?" Then the emperor's warriors fell before Devgeny, and he, with his lance and his sword, mowed them down like a good reaper. And on the first charge he defeated a thousand. Stepping back and charging anew, he defeated another thousand. And the Emperor Basil, on seeing Devgeny's valor, took a few warriors with him, and straightway took to flight. Of the other warriors Devgeny slew some and tied up the rest. Then Devgeny called to his companions: "Bring me my swift horse which is called Wind." And at once they brought him the swift horse. Mounting this, Devgeny pursued Basil, and caught up with him near the city. And he defeated the emperor's troops, and captured the emperor also.

56 Afterwards he sent a man into the city, and said: "You should tell the inhabitants of the city: 'Come out to receive Devgeny! God is pleased that I reign in your country today.'" When they heard this, the inhabitants of the city all gathered together, and went out of the city with the intention of fighting him, believing that they had to do with some ordinary man. Then Devgeny said to them: "Surrender your arms, and be angry no more!" And they answered: "You cannot quarrel with the whole city all yourself!" When Devgeny heard this he grew angry, and charged down on them, and some he slew, and others he tied up and turned over to his companions.

57 After this he entered the city and began to reign. After a little he released the prisoners, agreeing with the Scriptures that "the servant is not above his lord, nor is the son above the father." "And now I shall have twelve years of life, and I wish

to rest. The battles and the victories in which I succeeded in my youth were many." Saying this to his father, he placed him on the emperor's throne, and seated him. He sent for all his prisoners, and granted them their freedom. And only old Kinnamos and Ioannakes did he seal with his signet ring on the face, and sent them to their homes. And he gathered his household together, and held a big festival, and lived a long time.

Glory to God, now and forever, for ages upon ages. Amen.

Notes

G-i

[Separation of Proem from body of text, titles, book and section numbers, and summary added.]

[1-29] *[Proem]* A late addition in a different meter, the Byzantine development of the classical iambic trimeter. It can be read accentually as if written in trochaic hexameter; but examination will show that quantitatively iambics predominate. See *Tryp.*, pp. xi, xii.

[6] *Charziané* The military district of Charsianon was organized during the reign of Theophilus (829-42). See *CMH* vol. 4 pt. 2, p. 27 ff., and map, p. xlviii.

[12] *lands beside the sea* Possibly the Aegean coast, but perhaps more likely, the coast of modern Syria, Lebanon and Israel; the Crusaders' Outremer. See A 657 and T 202.

[21] *Both the all-glorious Theodores,* Until the time of Manuel Comnenus (1143-80) St. Theodore the Recruit and St. Theodore the Troop Commander were considered one and the same. See H. Delahaye's *Les Legendes Grecques des Saintes Militaires*: Paris, 109, S.V. "Theodore."

[25] *Demetrius* The patron saints of border troops, outlaws and soldiers were Demetrius, both Theodores, George and Mamas. See *Kal.* 2:4 21 n.

[45] *Turks, Dilemites* Turks were in growing demand as mercenaries. Dilemites were from Hyrcania. See *Gibbon*, 4, A. D. 549-556.

[46] *Troglodytes* Primitive people, mentioned solely for atmosphere, said to live on the coast of the Red Sea south of Egypt. See *OCD* S.V. "Troglodytes" and *Mav.*, pp. 4-5 n.

[50] *land of Heracles* Poeticism for the land around Cappadocian Heracleia, which is west of the Cilician Gates. See map, p. xlviii.

[57] *the General's house* As this is described as being in Cappadocia, the General must have been commander of the theme of that name.

[63] *in exile* Perhaps this is Andronicus Ducas who defected and fled to Baghdad in 806. See *CMH* vol. 4 pt. 1, 134-35, 716.

[70] *"O most belovéd children* She is unhappy not only because her

daughter is gone, but also because her *philotimo* (self esteem) has been offended. For a further discussion of this Greek characteristic, see Sanders, Irwin T. *Rainbow in the Rock.* Harvard, 1962, pp. 283-8.

[80] *cursed by me and by your father* The worst of all curses is a mother's.

[90] *Difficult* The Cilician Gates, a pass through the Taurus Mountains, See map, p. xlviii.

[101] *the Mosque* Mecca, then, as now, the most important mosque in the Moslem world. There must naturally have been a mosque in Palermo after it was taken by the Arabs in 831, but neither architecturally, sentimentally or religiously was it of importance. That the words *mosque* and *Palermo* occur in the same line means nothing, excepting possibly spite, because the city was now Moslem.

[102] *the Hanging Stone* Mosque of Omar in Jerusalem, known also as the Dome of the Rock because it covers the rock from which Mohammed ascended to heaven. The idea of hanging probably comes from the small treasury adjacent, known as the Dome of the Chain; its gate was guarded by a chain.

[103] *the Prophet's Tomb* In Medina.

[104] *the sacred prayer* "There is no God but God, and Mohammed is His Prophet."

[115] *the Roman tongue* At this time Greek was the tongue of the Eastern Roman Empire.

[120] *single combat* The offer of single combat recalls *Arab. Nts.,* p. 161.

[161-74] See also *Arab. Nts.,* p. 190, for single combat, costumes and situation.

[263] *"Whose sons . . . are you?"* The genealogy quiz can be found as far back as Homer. See *Il.* G. 123. It is characteristically Greek.

[265] *from the Anatolic Theme* The General's house was in the Cappadocian military district (which became a theme), but the brothers are claiming descent from a family of the Anatolic (of which the Cappadocian had formerly been a part) because its General ranked ahead even of the Domesticus of the Scholarii, who, in the tenth century at least, took supreme command of the army when the Emperor himself was not present in the field. Thus they were from the very highest social class. See *CMH* vol. 4, part 2, p. 39, and map therein, p. 48.

[287] *Our mother a Ducas* One of the most prominent of the Byzantine noble families. The Constantine to whom she is kin might be any one of several—all improbable from a historical point of view: Constantine Ducas, Domestic of the Schools, who, however, appears to be her son; the Emperor Constantine X Ducas (1059-67), or his son, or nephew. The *Kinnamades* have not been identified. See *CMH* vol. 4, pt. 1, pp. 134, 793.

²⁷⁰ *Our father's exiled* If this is Andronicus Ducas, his sons would certainly prefer to say that he was "exiled" rather than that he had defected. See note, 1. 63 above.

²⁸⁴ *Chrysoverges* In A and T he is called Chrysocherpes. There is no name in history (except for the Patriarch Nicholas II Chrysoverges) that so closely resembles Chrysocheir, the leader of the Paulician heresy, as these. It cannot be the Patriarch, but his name may have been borrowed. See *CMH* vol. 4, pt. 1, pp. 119-20, 714, and *Gibbon*, V.

²⁸⁸ *Who brought me up* I have used Sathas and Legrand's reading (see *Mav.*, p. 19, n.) here because the text makes little sense.

²⁹⁵ *Amorium up to Iconium,* Coming from Cappadocian Heracleia (or even from Pontic Heracleia), one reaches Iconium before Amorium, and not after. *Mav.* suggests that the name Akroinon is concealed here, but Akroinon was a defeat for the Arabs; their leader, Saïd Battal, was killed here in 740. See *CMH* vol. 4, pt. 1, pp. 64, 699.

³⁰⁶ *come to Romania* Change allegiance; Abu Hafs changed allegiance in 928.

³³² *the power of passion* The text reads, "the Romans' power," which is grammatically correct. But the scribe evidently forgot the point of the story. I have used the reading of A and T. See *Mav.*, p. 23, 332 n.

G-ii

[*Title precedes book number in ms.; summary added.*]

²⁶ *while she rejoiced* It is possible, but unnecessary to imagine a lyric at this point; the song she has been singing is told in ll. 16-25. She is rejoicing, in spite of her worries, because family honor is to be saved by the marriage.

⁶⁰ *your father's deeds* The event described resembles the defeat of Amr, emir of Melitene, by Petronas in 863. See *CMH* vol. 4, pt. 1, p. 713. It also might be a combination of Chrysocheir's raids on Ephesus, Ancyra, and his defeat and beheading at Tephrike in 872. See *CMH* vol 4, pt., pp 119-20. The text of E is cautious, mentions both father and grandfather, but not by name, and mentions one place Chrysocheir did raid, Nicomedeia. The other places named in E are obscure: Ammos might be Amisus, raided by Amr on his last and fatal expedition; it could hardly be Amasea, which was not involved at that time. Perneton can hardly be Pergamum, for that had not been raided since 717. See *CMH* vol. 4, pt. 1, pp. 62, 698.

⁶⁹ *Master of Horse* Protostrator originally meant Chief of the Grooms. Philotheus, writing in 899, describes this as one of the "special offices" of considerable importance. By the thirteenth century it meant "com-

[137]

protostrator", vol. 4, pt. 2, p. 27, and *Gean.*, p. 420.

[75] *Mourses Karoës* Only one uncle is mentioned here, but in A and T there are two, Mousour Tarsites and Karoës; and two in E, Mouratasites and Karoïles, both corruptions of the two in A and T. Mourses may be a corruption of Mousour, and Mousour is probably a corruption of Mansour, Arabic for Victorious, the appelation of two caliphs and the family name of St. John Damascene. If this is so, Mousour Tarsites may be the Victorious Tarsite, which would surely be Ali ibn Yahya, emir of Tarsus. Karoës is usually identified with the Paulician Karbeas, but might be Karghuyeh, known also as Karoës, who surrendered Aleppo to the Byzantines in 969-70. See *CMH* vol. 4, pt. 1, pp. 111, 712-13.

[76] *Led raids* The places raided, and the texts in which these names occur are as follows: unidentifiable places are shown in parentheses: Abydus, G; (Akina, A, T); (Ammos, E); Ancyra, G, A, T: Armenia, E; (Hermonus, E); Konion, E; Nicomedeia, E; (Perneton, E); (Seven Towns, A. T.); (Six Towns, G.); Taranda, G, A, T; Tephrike, G, A, T; (Zygos, E). The identification of the raider is nearly impossible. Three men, however, made raids of importance Ali ibn Yahya, whose raid in 853 nearly reached Constantinople (*CMH* vol. 4, pt. 1, p. 712); Amr, the emir of Melitene, whose raid in 863 resulted in his death, and Chrysocheir, who reached Ephesus in 853.

[78] *Tephrike* In G, A and T the name is written Aphrike, an obvious error. Tephrike was the headquarters of the Paulician sect, and in the middle of the territory where the action occurs.

[82] *swine-eater* Christian; Mohammedans do not eat pork.

[98] *then be cursed!"* A mother's curse. See G-i 80.

[101] *Lakkopetra* Leukoptra in A and T; Chalkopetris and Chalkopetron in E. According to *Kal.*, 1:47, 680 n, Savvas Ioannides located this place in the plain of Chariana between the Antitaurus and Parnadros Mountains; there is a hill of white rock thought by local inhabitants to be the site of Digenis's house. Leukopetra means "white stone", but Lakkopetra means a stone marking a hollow place, or tank.

[135] *a dream* See OCD, S.V. Divination.

[157] *"Welcome . . .* Custom demands that they accept hospitality.

[208] *the three mile mark* This distance is repeated in G-iv 800, G-v 100, and A 2590 (as a correction from T 1702). *Kal.*, index, suggests that this is the last military landmark, or limit of surveillance. *Mav.*, p. 43 n, finds evidence of this distance in Persian usage as early as

the fourth century. It would appear to be the forerunner of our three-mile-limit at sea.

G-iii

[*Title precedes book number in ms.; Emir's added to title, and summary added.*]

[50] *Rachav* Rachas and Rache in E, but Rouchas in A and T, assumed to be Edessa, because it was in Edessa that the Sacred Towel of Abgar was kept. But see l. 150 n below. It is not impossible that Raqqa, Haroun-al-Raschid's headquarters on the Euphrates, directly south of Edessa, may be meant.

[67] *Mellokopia* Called Mylokopodin in A, Mylokopia in E. The battle in which Amr was killed in 863 was south of the Halys River, near Malakopia.

[92] *a fearsome lion* Lions have been seen near Damascus as recently as 1880. See A. B. Meyer's "The Antiquity of the Lion in Greece," translated from *Zoologischer Garten* in *Annual Report of the Board of Regents, Smithsonian Institution, for 1903*, Washington, D. C., 1904.

[121] *in boots* Only the Emperor wore red boots. No color is mentioned here, but high rank seems to be implied.

[150] *the Towel of Naaman* Two stories about the cure of leprosy are involved here: (1) Naaman, captain of the Syrian host, was cured of leprosy by Elisha, who told him to bathe seven times in the Jordan. The towel he used became a relic; (2) Abgar V, King of Osroene (Edessa), wrote Jesus, requesting a visit and a cure for leprosy. The letter Jesus sent in reply, and the piece of linen he sent with the impression of his face both became relics. The Sacred Towel of Abgar was taken to Constantinople in 944. The Sacred Letter is supposed to have remained until the fall of Edessa in 1032. What became of the Towel of Naaman is uncertain. Although the stories of Naaman and Abgar are separated by many centuries, they were confused, for Edessa was the center of the trade in relics. It should be noted, however, that the Emir's mother does not say that she was herself in Edessa, nor that she herself had the relic, but only that the towel was "with us," or "belonged to us," that is, to the Moslems. See 2 *Kings* 5; 1-14; *Enc. Brit.*, S.V. *Abgar; CMH* vol. 4, pt. 1, pp. 718, 725; *Gibbon*, V.

[308] *hunt the partridge* Find a bride?

[327] *the horses pranced* This agrees with the ms. Legrand, *Dig. Acr.*, 1902, has unnecessarily changed the verb to "whinnied," in his critical note.

G-iv

[*Title and summary added.*]

27   *Achilles*   Probably the Homeric hero; but possibly the poet had the Byzantine romance *The Achilleïd* in mind.

28–32   *Alexander*   The characterization does not fit the historical Alexander of Macedon; the name was known principally from the pseudo-Callisthenes' *Romance of Alexander* and its many translations and recensions.

33   *old Philopappos*   The name has been borrowed from that of one of the kings of ancient Commagene, which lay to the west of the Euphrates near Samosata, its capital. The monument of Philopappos in Athens was erected in honor of the grandson of the last king. The appearance of the name in the poem suggests that parts of the poem have been derived from legends of these kings. See *OCD* S.V. "Philopappos"; *Mav.* p. lxix; and *E* 1320.

33–34   *Ioannakes/*, or *Kinnamos*   Ioannakes and variants of this name all mean Johnnie. *Kal.*, 1:75, note on A 1333, suggests that this is a name from Commagene. Both of these men are sons, or at least relatives, of Philopappos.

38   *Three thousand chosen lancers*   Repeated from G-i 291, and therefore a clue to oral composition.

39   *Kufah*   The first Abbasid was hailed as Caliph by his troops here in 749. See *CMH* vol. 4, pt. 1, pp. 638, 786. See map, p. xlviii. This reference helps date the composition of the story.

54   *Antakinos*   The General (G-i 57). Called Aaron (A 22; E 145), and Andronicus (A 23). Usually identified with Andronicus Ducas (see *CMH* vol. 4, pt. 1, pp. 130, 131, 716). The name Antakinos comes from the Turkish epic, *Saïd Battal*, in which a Greek general is called Antaki-Kafir, that is, the Infidel from Antioch. See *Kal.* 2:37, 54 n.

56   *Basil the Blessèd*   The emperor who exiled the General is named Romanus in all versions except this and the Slavic. Historically it was Leo VI who became emperor at the time Andronicus Ducas defected.

199   *breast like crystal*   Description applied to the Emperor Constantine IX Monomachus by the historian Psellus. See *Mav.* p. lxxxi; and *Kal.*, 1:42, 199 n.

217   *they drank thirstily*   This idea has survived into the present century among schoolboys at boardingschool, but in the opposite sense: anyone who would drink his own bath water must be a revolting creature.

341   *ignoble things*   Such was the seclusion in which girls were kept, that even speaking face to face was considered improper.

351–56   *For rays of light rose up out of her face*   The description is derived from *Ach. Tat.*, 1.4.3.

380   *he could eat no food*   He was still young, being only twelve or fif-

teen years old, and he was badly smitten. This is one of the more human touches in the poem.

[398] *At first he touched the strings* Description similar to *Ach. Tat.*, 1.5.4.

[858] *three thousand* See above, G-i 790.

[905] *Abasgia* Georgian kingdom at the eastern end of the Black Sea. See map, p. xlviii.

[912] *Chosroës* Probably Chosroës II, King of Persia. He was defeated by the Emperor Heraclius in 627. See *CMH* vol. 4, pt. 1, p. 605.

[965] *outlaws* The Greek word, *apelates*, means "drivers-away," i.e., cattle-rustlers. See *Soph.* S.V. "apelates."

[969] *Mavrochionites* Probably the same as Mavronites (G-iii 205) and Mavrioroi (A 4636). *Mav.*, p. 133 n, suggests a relationship to Mavron Oros (Black Mountain), between Antioch and the sea. This might be a spur of Mt. Casius at the mouth of the Orontes; the people referred to would actually be Antiochenes.

[970] *Ethiops* Dark-skinned people. Both those of India as well as those from Ethiopia and other parts of Africa, were all called Ethiops.

[975] *Persians* The natives of eastern countries were called Persians indiscriminately.

[980] *"We've learned* It was customary for the Emperor to refer to himself in the first person plural, just as it was for Queen Victoria in modern times. The poet, being a provincial, and obviously unfamiliar with court procedure, has the Emperor call himself "my majesty." In English such terminology sounds slightly ridiculous. As the author obviously intended no ridicule, I have translated by using the customary modern words. The same words occur in the Slavic version, but as ridicule seems to be intended there, I have not changed the terminology.

[1044] *tribute* There seems to be no evidence that Iconium ever paid tribute to the Emperor. The reference is obscure.

[1050] *your grandfather's estates* When Antakinos was exiled—or defected—his estates were confiscated. See notes on G-i 63, 270; and G-iv 54.

[1055] *wild, unbroken horses* The Emperor Basil I the Macedonian had done the same thing. See *Gibbon*, V.

G-v

[*Title and Summary added.*]

[20] *fairly* Neither boasting of nor suppressing facts.

[24] *fifteen years* Literally, in his fifteenth year; we should say he was still fourteen.

[51] *consolation* In a world of strict seclusion of women, she was asking for trouble—and got it.

[64] "*We sat together*   For a picture of this scene and of Basil himself, see *CMH* vol. 4, pt. 2, plates 40 and 41.

[66] *Meferkéh*   Mayyafariqin, or Martyropolis.

[67] *Happlorabdes*   Possibly Abu Taghlib, emir of Mosul, who paid tribute to John Tzimisces in 972. See *CMH* vol. 4, pt. 1, p. 723.

[100] *three mile mark*   See G-ii 298; G-iv 800.

[165] *Blattolivadi*   Translated "purple meadow." This same episode occurs in A 2659. But see G-viii 81 and A 4445; both imply that the episode of the dragon and the lion (G-vi 42 ff, and A 2838) occurred here also. This is possible, but the place is not named at the time of the episode—only in the recapitulation in the death scene.

[168] *Mousou*   This is the third of three people given this name: (1) the Emir himself (in A); (2) the Emir's uncle (in A); and (3) a highwayman (here and in A). Except for the possibility of confusion, there is no reason why a highwayman might not have been called "victorious." See note on G-ii 75.

[223] *Ethiops' faith*   This reference suggests that the girl herself might have been dark-skinned.

[231] "*When I heard this*   It is curious that adultery with a pagan was considered worse than with a Christian.

[259] *General Antiochus*   Unidentified.

[263] *lawbreaker*   The author has merged two separate scenes here: (1) when Basil rescues the boy; and (2) later, when he gives the girl back to the boy. He could not have known the boy was a lawbreaker during the first scene.

G-vi
[*Title and Summary added.*]

[4-11] *a king of months*   See *Ach. Tat.* 2.1.2., where the rose is the king of flowers.

[15-41] *And so when. . . . cheerfulness*   See *Ach. Tat.* 1.15.1-8. The garden scenes in Books vi and vii contain many lines that are duplicated. These are not examples of oral tradition, for they all come directly from *Ach. Tat.* 15.1-8. Lines 18, 19, 20, 22, 23, 24, 25, 26, 27, and 28 appear in G-vii as 21, 30, 31, 37, 39, 38, 40, 41, 34, and 33. The difference in order suggests that they were memorized but not repeated in correct order.

[47] *A dragon*   The word might be translated as "serpent," but the beast is more magical and romantic than the serpent in *Il.* 2.308 ff.

[65] *three large heads*   Even Homeric serpents sometimes had three heads. See *Il.* 11.39.

[109] *when the girl said 'rose'*   See *Ach. Tat.* 2.1.3.

[117] *Trosis*   The word means "wounding" (see L-S-J). Said to be a place now called Trusch. (See *Mav.*, p. 168 n.)

¹²⁰⁻²² *They . . . . the third*   These lines clearly belong between lines 180-81, where I have placed them.

¹⁴⁰ *my voice died*   Copied exactly from *Ach. Tat.* 3.11.2. with only a possessive pronoun added.

¹⁴³ *"Whom God hath joined*   See *Matthew* 19:6. The words are almost identical; the differences are significant, and can be found by comparing the translation with the King James Version.

³⁶¹ *the beacon*   See *CMH* vol. 4, pt. 2, pp. 38, 43, 50, 304, for the military signaling system of the Empire.

³⁸⁵ *Maximo.*   The Amazons have always come from just beyond the limits of the known world. The Alexander is, of course, that of The Alexander Romance, not history.

³⁹⁸ *irregulars*   Outlaws would hardly ward off irregulars, but it is possible that this episode is derived from some legend of Commagene in which King Philopappos's troops are fighting their own variety of outlaws.

⁴²⁷ *Melementzes*   Maximo's chief lieutenant. The name is spelled variously, but this way seems best because there are today tribes of nomads in S. E. Turkey who are known as "Sons of Melemenji." See *Kal.*, 1:189, note on A 3400, and *Mav.*, p. liii. Melementzes has been plausibly identified with Melias, or Mleh the Great, an Armenian soldier who became general of the theme of Lycandus, south of Charsianon and east of Cappadocia, during the reign of Constantine VII Porphyrogenitus.

⁴³³ *dainty fare*   The girl.

⁵⁴⁹ *Leander*   He appears here for the first time, and when he falls to earth in line 629 he disappears from the story. He probably belongs to the legend of Commagene which brought Philopappos into the story.

⁵⁵⁰ *whipping*   The Greek word is obscure, but judging from *Soph.* S.V. "charzánion," literally, "in strap fashion," that is, swinging from side to side.

⁵⁶⁹⁻⁷¹ *'Maximo . . . proper.'*   See *Arab. Nts.*, p. 162. The Greek poet here gives a lesson in manners to his Arabian counterpart.

⁶⁴⁶ *lived to flee*   The derivation is clear, even though the sense has been warped: "For he who fights and comes away/may live to fight another day;" a saying that goes back to Archilochus.

⁷⁸²⁻⁸⁴ *Maximo's tunic*   See *Ach. Tat.*, 1.1.11.

⁷⁸⁵⁻⁸²⁷ [A page has been torn from the ms. here. The story can be followed by inserting A 3802-3842. It should be noted, however, that the language of the Grottaferrata and Andros versions is different, that each poem was composed by a different singer, and that the result is like inserting lines of Portuguese in a Spanish poem. This difference, of course, cannot be made noticeable in translation without resorting to

ridiculous English that would falsify the poem completely. I have inserted it here solely for the sake of the story which must have been much the same in both versions, although we cannot prove it.]

786-87 [The ms. resumes the story at l. 786, but l. 787 should not be next; the sense is incomplete. We have therefore inserted A 3844 and A 3845 between, and then resumed the story.]

G-vii

[*Title and summary added.*]

21-41 *Tall reeds* Repeated, word for word, from G-vi 18. Many other lines follow closely those in G-vi. The source for both passages is *Ach. Tat.* 1.15.1-8.

51 *And cross-shaped halls* I have followed the reading suggested in *Mav.*, p. 218-219 n. Cross-shaped statues (crucifixes?) are not logical here; but five square cubicles form a Greek cross, the most common form for a Byzantine church, and the word suggested means dining hall.

85 *Achilles' fabled wars* Clearly the poet knew little of Homer or the Homeric stories. He was more at home when referring to characters in the Alexander romance, from which came Candace, the Brahmans, and the Amazons.

105 *Theodore* Just one is mentioned here, indicating that the text was probably first written before the middle of the twelfth century, and that when two Theodores are mentioned, the text had been amended to bring it up to current belief.

136 *for a moment* This is classical usage of the preposition. *Mav.* p. 224 n, has missed it. See *L-S-J*, S.V. *pará*," C, II, 10, d.

208 *those descended from slaves* The Arabs.

209 *children of the free* The Greeks. For this thought and that of the preceding line, see *Bowra*, p. 14.

221 *war in general* See Matthew 24:6.

G-viii

[*Title precedes book number in ms; summary added.*]

6 *The cause of it occurring in the bath* Alexander the Great suffered cramps and fever from bathing in the river Cydnus. See *Arr. Anab.*, 2:4, 7-8.

36 *lumbago* The symptoms described might mean meningitis, tetanus, or strychnine poisoning, but are still too vague to diagnose with certainty. I have therefore used a word equally vague to translate the Greek word.

54 *army doctors* For Byzantine medical practice see *CMH* vol. 4, pt. 2, p. 43, 289-92.

146 [The word "Mistress" omitted in translation. It was used in reference to the Theotokos at the Council of Constantinople in A.D. 536, ac-

[144]

cording to *Soph.* S.V. "despoina"—4; see also p. ix S.V. Const. (536) *Mav.* l. 3683 n (p. 241) seems to have misread this.

²⁰⁵ *Buccellariots, Podandites* The text reads Kukulithariots and Kondandites, both obvious misspellings.

²⁰⁶ *Mavronites* See note on G-iv 969. Bathyrryakites are traced by *Mav.* l. 3741 n (p. 245) to Anna Commena's *Alexiad*, 2.6.30.

²³⁹ *Trosis* See note on G-vi 117.

²⁴⁰ *standing upon an arch* This might be a triumphal arch, but is more likely to be the arch of a bridge. See E 1660.

A-i

[*Titles added*]

[*The story of Basil's mother*]

"*From Eustathius to a certain Manuel,*" Eustathius might, at most, be the name of the redactor. No significance has been attached to the name Manuel.

¹⁴ *Anatolian* The East, Asia Minor; not the Anatolic Theme.

¹⁷⁻¹⁸ *lords . . . king* These are folktale titles, and the word "emperor" is not the right translation here.

²⁰⁻²³ *Ducas . . . Aaron . . . Andronicus* See note on *Antakinos*, G-iv 54.

²⁹ *Magastrani* Elsewhere Magastri or Kyr Magastri. Unidentified.

³⁰ *Anna.* Unidentified; a common Byzantine name.

³⁴ *they lacked a girl* A rare complaint; grief over childlessness or lack of a boy was normal.

A-1

⁴¹ *a seer* Possibly from *Barlaam and Ioasaph*, 3.19.

⁴³ [A garbled mixture of 42 and 43. Perhaps the scribe whom the poet was dictating to became confused. Omitted.]

⁵⁶ *a marvelous place* See *St. J*, 3.20.

⁶² [Line confused. Omitted.]

⁶⁸ *Irene* No name given to her in G. Perhaps, because her name means Peace, she was given it for her supposed influence for peace. Probably she was given it simply because so many women in the Byzantine court had the name.

⁹⁰ *three thousand Saracens old soldiers,* Here again the number three thousand occurs, see G-i 291, G-iv 38, etc. The word I have translated as "soldiers" means, according to *Kal.* 2:18 n, "bodyguards," which fits the context, but the explanation, taken from Henri Gregoire, is unsatisfactory. The word is said to occur in the *Chanson de Roland* in the form "açopars." I have yet to find it in Bedier's edition, but I do find "açopail," a failure, and "açopeor," that which fails, in Godefroy, *Lexique de l'Ancien Français*. This is not helpful.

⁹⁸ *an inner garden* See *Ach. Tat.* 1.15.1-8. Also See *Sherrard*, p. 58, on the mechanical birds in the throne room of the Magnaura Palace, built by Leo the Mathematician for the Emperor Theophilus.

A-i

100a [A line is missing here, for the following lines need some connecting link in order to make sense. I have made a tentative restoration.]

104 [This line has been removed and placed after 121 where it fits.]

124 *the age of twelve*   She is younger than Shakespeare's Juliet.

133 *Her face . . .*   The description of Irene could be taken from any of the Hellenistic romances.

161-67 See *Ach. Tat.* 1.1.13. The painting is the same.

184 *threefold slave*   See *Ach. Tat.* 8.1.2, and note 2.

261-78 [These lines are roughly eight syllable iambic rhymed couplets, each couplet written as one line. As rhyme was not in general use before the fifteenth century, these lines are a late interpolation.]

A-ii

290-300 *Her father'd . . . place*   Borrowed from the story of Nausicaa in *Od.* 6.57-84.

A-iv

[*A visit with Philopappos*]

1566-1673 If this episode is not a late interpolation, it belongs immediately after G-iv 253. To me, however, that placement seems out of character with the G version.

A-v

[*The blinded cook*]

2322-2333 This piece of unnecessary brutality is out of character. *Mav.* p. xl finds a source in one of Alexander's acts.

A-vii

[*The story of Ancylas*]

3066-3120 The story is pointless, added only to remind the reader that the Border Lord is, after all, human.

E

[*Beginning of the Escorial Version*]

1-17 This sample offers no new episodes, but shows, by contrast, how confused and irregular this version is. In language it is more demotic than G, A or T, but its repeated lines and phrases seem to come from the confused efforts of an ignorant scribe to take dictation he did not understand.

Sb

[*Defeat of the Emperor Basil*]

48-57 Digenis appears here under his Russian name, Devgeny. It should be noted that this is the only version except G in which the emperor's name is Basil; elsewhere he is Romanus. As this is a translation from another translation, which may have been a translation too, not too much attention need be paid to it. The atmosphere, however, certainly seems that of folktale. Its principal interest is that it shows how far the stories of Digenis Akritas spread.

Works Consulted

Lexicons

L-S-J Liddell, Henry George, B. D.; Scott, Robert, D.D.; Jones, Sir Henry Stuart. *Greek-English Lexicon.* 9th. ed. Oxford: The Clarendon Press, 1940.

Soph. Sophocles, E. A. *Greek Lexicon of the Roman and Byzantine Periods.* 2 vols, 1887. Reprint. New York: Frederick Ungar Publishing Co.

Histories

Gibbon Gibbon, Edward. *The History of the Decline and Fall of the Roman Empire.* Ed. by William Smith. 6 vols. New York: Bigelow, Brown and Co., Inc., n.d. There are so many editions of Gibbon that it is impossible to give more than volume and chapter numbers for references.

CMH Hussey, J. M., ed. *The Byzantine Empire.* Vol. 4. The Cambridge Medieval History. Cambridge: at the University Press, 1967.

References

Ach. Tat. Tatius, Achilles. *Leucippe and Cleitophon.* Edited and translated by S. Gaselee. Loeb Classical Library, 1962.

Arr. Anab. Arrian, *Anabasis Alexandri, Indica.* Edited and translated by E. Iliff Robson. 2 vols. Loeb Classical Library, 1954.

Arab. Nts. Campbell, Joseph, ed. *The Portable Arabian Nights.*

New York: The Viking Press, 1952. Thirty-six complete stories from John Payne's edition of 1881, and the rest in epitome.

Hadas, Moses. *Three Greek Romances.* Garden City, N. Y.: Doubleday Co., 1953. Contains Longus's *Daphnis and Chloe,* Xenophon of Ephesus's *An Ephesian Tale,* and Dio Chrysostom's *The Hunters of Euboea* in English.

Haight, Elizabeth. *Essays on the Greek Romances.* Port Washington, N. J.: Kennikat Press, 1943. Contains epitomes in English of Chariton's *Chaereas and Callirhoe,* Xenophon of Ephesus's *An Ephesian Tale,* Heliodorus's *Aethiopica,* and Achilles Tatius's *Leucippe and Cleitophon.*

Heliodorus. *Aethiopica.* Budé: Paris, 1953.

St. J. St. John Damascene. *Barlaam and Ioasaph.* Edited and translated by G. R. Woodward and H. Mattingly. Loeb Classical Library, 1962.

Longus. *Daphnis and Chloe.* Translated by George Thornley, rev. by J. M. Edmonds. Loeb Classical Library, 1916.

Tryp. Trypanis, C. A. *Medieval and Modern Greek Poetry.* Oxford: The Clarendon Press, 1951-64. Poetry in Greek, introduction in English.

The reader is also recommended to consult The Bible, Authorized version; *I Kaini Diathíki,* The New Testament authorized by the Orthodox Church of Greece; Homer's *Iliad,* edited by D. B. Monroe and T. W. Allen, Oxford Classical Texts, 3d ed., 1959; and Homer's *Odyssey,* edited by T. W. Allen, Oxford Classical Texts, 2d ed., 1959.